KINGDOM'S ADVENT

Kingdom Fantasy Short Stories

Jim Doran

ISBN: 978-0-9601017-1-9 (sc)
ISBN: 978-0-9601017-0-2 (e)

Cover design by: Daniel Johnson
Library of Congress Control Number: 2020905570
Printed in the United States of America

For Francis E. Doran, USMC

CONTENTS

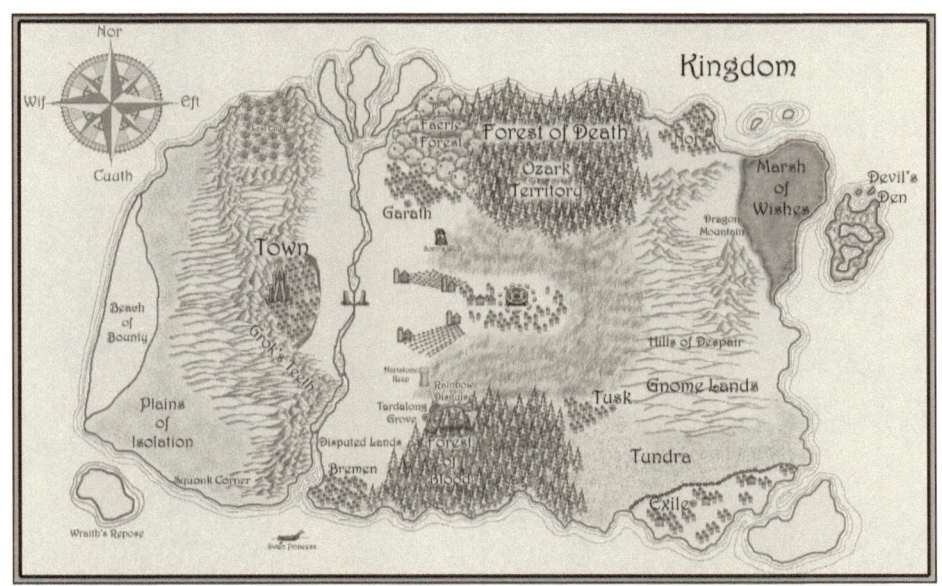

AERON'S CHOICE

Once upon a time, there was a magical city named Exile with a magical border, magical creatures, and magical residents, most of whom were criminals. In the fantasy world of Kingdom, the rulers deemed sentencing felons to dungeons in the nobility's neighborhoods unwise. The king himself was informed of men and women who had committed murder, plunder, forbidden sorcery, and crimes against the crown. He sent them away to Exile, far from his castles where the lawbreakers, free to roam that city but not to leave it, established their lives and businesses.

On one particular day then, a blameless resident of Exile moved along a thoroughfare, passing a milliner's, a pawnbroker's, and a grocery store—each building pressed against the next, much as fish packed together for sale. Here, stairs led to second-story shops, these slightly shadier than the ground floor establishments.

The street in front meandered in a circuitous route like

every other lane in this neighborhood, leaving no room for any quiet place of solitude.

The girl, that guiltless child, waved to the barber sharpening his razors. He had killed many elves in cold blood, but his haircuts were the best in Exile. Next door, Ms. Willbell, who ran a fruit store, greeted the girl. Rumors said the king had banished the produce seller here because she'd worked in the king's castle and "knew too much."

The child hadn't passed anyone her own age this entire morning. The only young people in Exile were those who'd had to accompany their parents to serve out their sentences. Innocents didn't last long here.

The girl had staked out a corner outside of the haymarket. Her thin, eleven-year-old frame fit snugly between the barrels that acted as both tables and a storefront. Her father sent her out at the start of every day to collect firewood to sell—their only source of income. Every morning, she awoke before the sun came up. She never ate breakfast. Instead, she walked a little beyond the border of Exile, gathered wood others couldn't reach, and carried it back.

Being free of fault, the girl passed outside of Exile's boundaries without consequence, giving her an advantage when collecting her wares. She lugged the wood to the center of the square nearest her father's home and sold it all day, hoping to make enough money to buy her father and herself a meal. And so her life went, day after day, the gathering, the selling, and if she was lucky, the dining.

The child never thought of having a different life or routine. She had lived in Exile since she was four years old, when her father had been arrested. While she didn't exactly love her father, her sense of duty linked them together, and joined her to her job as a woodseller. She never thought of running away or exploring any more of Kingdom.

Arms full of wood, she was hurrying toward her spot when she nearly walked straight into an older boy rounding a corner in front of her. He appeared so suddenly she dropped some of the logs and tree limbs in her hands. Instead of assisting her, the boy leaned against a brick wall and crossed his arms. "I have seen you before. You are the young wood peddler." He spoke as any Kingdom native would—formally, without contractions.

Eyes glued to him in case he made a sudden move, the girl bent her knees. "How gentlemanly of you not to assist," she couldn't help but say.

"In this city, 'tis suspicious. Many pickpockets roam these streets."

The girl scooped up a heavy branch and put it on her pile. "Are you a pickpocket?"

He ignored her question. "I have observed you hawking your wares. You will never sell much wood that way."

She scrunched her cheeks together in an annoyed expression that hid her freckles. "I suppose you know of a better method?"

"Indeed."

She retrieved the last of the wood. "And you will not share it? Customary in this town, I suppose."

The boy said, "My name is Aeron. Yours?"

She was cautious. Not many in this place were kind, and she preferred her anonymity. However, she decided to take the risk and answer him. "Valencia."

He bowed slightly. "If you say 'wood for sale,' they will not listen. You have to tell them why they want the wood. Remind them that they need some light, or they need to cook their meals. Predict a storm—tell them they require the wood or they shall find themselves chilled to the bone."

"But no storm approaches."

Aeron scanned the sky, looking from one direction to the other, revealing a teardrop-shaped birthmark under his chin. "They do not know that."

"'Tis wicked to lie."

"It is also wicked to let us starve, but many here would do so. They will eventually use the wood. And perhaps your prognostics will be true. Exile sees its share of winter."

Valencia considered his proposition. The nights grew longer at this time of the year, and people truly would need the wood for light and heat to cook their meals. The snow, too, would come soon enough. She wasn't a liar, though. She knew if she tried to fib or even exaggerate the truth, she would begin to stutter and embarrass herself.

Aeron stepped forward. "How about this? Allow me to do the selling and leave you to collect the money. At the end of the day, we will share it. For every three coins, you shall receive one."

"'Tis hardly a fair bargain," objected Valencia. "How about we trade off each coin, and if we take in an odd amount, you may keep the extra?"

Aeron extended his hand. "'Tis an honorable pact."

Valencia, her arms full of wood, brushed the edge of his fingers with her own.

The rest of the day, Aeron pitched the merits of firewood as if it were a gift from the heavens, and Valencia passed cords to eagerly awaiting customers. Noticing the bundle dwindle to nearly nothing, Aeron sent Valencia to gather more as he sold the last of their stock. Valencia counted the remaining logs, and when she returned, they were all gone, but not Aeron. She handed her wares to the customers in the queue for their goods.

Valencia marveled at the boy's guile, his effortless pitches, his ability to pick out a person from a crowd who would purchase their wood. But she told herself she refused to admire him.

After they depleted their inventory a second time, Aeron lifted the pouch containing the day's profits and shook it. A metallic, hollow jingle rang down the street, a sound that would set rapacious moneylenders salivating. Valencia silently cursed herself. Why had she trusted him with the coins? She should have demanded it as she passed out the wood. Now he would take it all for himself.

"A fine day's work. Do you wish to count the profits in order to ensure I did not cheat you?"

Valencia held out her hand and he placed the money pouch in her long fingers. Slowly, she counted the coins twice and kept her half. "It has been a fine day."

"I think fortune favors us. Shall we meet here tomorrow?"

Valencia shook the coins in her apron pocket. "I thank you for your advice and assistance today."

"We make good confederates." He winked.

"You have committed no crime and could pass Exile's borders," she said. "Why do you need me? You could collect the wood yourself."

He shrugged. "And now, observing me, you could sell the wood yourself. Yet you know good wood from bad. Many have commented on the quality of our stock. I do not believe I would fare as well."

"And I could copy your methods, but it does not suit me."

Aeron bowed slightly. "Colleagues?"

Valencia curtsied back. "*D'accord!*" She agreed.

When Valencia brought her coins home to her father, she thought he would be pleased with the windfall jangling in her small pocket. They would be able to eat tonight, possibly something better than stew made from the discarded bones of small game birds.

Valencia's father, indeed, accepted the coins with both hands and counted them. She beamed at him then as he planted the metal pieces in small piles on their lopsided table.

Her father's wiry frame shifted uncomfortably. "Did you steal it?"

Valencia placed her hand on her chest. "No! I would never steal."

"You are an urchin. Stealing is a street child's way of life."

"Not mine."

Her father said, "Precisely why we starve. What did you do today to collect this money? You did not do something else you ought not?"

Valencia didn't know what he meant, but his squinting

right eye made her nervous. He examined the buttons on her ragged blouse. She placed her hands behind her back. "I met a boy. He helped sell my wood."

Her father's eyes narrowed. "Who is this boy?"

"His name is Aeron."

"The fourteen-year-old hoodlum with the straight teeth? You are a fool. Do you not know anything?"

"Why?"

"His father is a murderer, and his mother is a thief. Coming from those two, he will be nothing but trouble. Stay away from him!"

"But, Father, we made so much money."

The instant she said it, she regretted her words. She had broken one of her father's cardinal rules. Never disagree. His jaw set, and she anticipated his next move.

"Hands!"

She put her hands down on the table.

Her father's arm darted out, his arm cuff glinting in the candlelight, and grabbed a switch from the windowsill. He used it twice on each of her hands. The punishing strikes stung, but Valencia had been through this many times before. Two swats were light punishment to her now.

Her father set the switch back on the windowsill. "I will not have you associating with that boy."

Valencia believed her father invented rules she didn't understand to safeguard her. Slight for her age, she trusted that her father simply wanted the best for her. He protected her in this dangerous town, the only one who would, and she was stupid to disobey. Therefore, when he said he used the switch to remind her, she believed him without question.

Valencia ran to the butcher shop and bought two pigeons. Her father cooked them into a chunky soup. She went to bed with a stomach full of the bird instead of the frequent discomfort of hunger. And before she climbed into her pile of straw with the tattered cloth she used as a blanket, she knelt down to pray.

"I am sorry I worked with Aeron today. As father said, I

should know better. Sometimes, I listen to my common sense when I should not. Born of two terrible people, Aeron must be a terrible person himself. Please protect me, your loving little child."

The next day, Valencia returned to her location, and with a trembling heart, began to expound the virtues of the wood, trying to mimic Aeron's technique. Most people quickly rushed past without even noticing the girl's weak voice and uninspired style. When Aeron appeared, he greeted her with a sly grin. "Early start? We shall run out of wood again with such a little pile."

Valencia ignored him and presented a stick of wood to Mr. Marnes, the landlord who had once set his neighbor's house on fire.

Aeron waved his hand in front of her face. "Valencia? Do you hear me? Did a witch cast an invisibility spell on me?"

"I am not allowed to talk to you."

Aeron stuck out his lower lip in mock hurt. "What happened?"

Valencia said, "My father told me your father is a murderer and your mother is a thief."

"True. They are other things as well."

"Then you are no good."

Aeron leaned against the wall. "Because of my parents?"

Valencia nodded and called out to a passerby, pointing at her wood.

Aeron blew his black bangs out of his eyes. "Do you believe I am a bad person?"

"What I believe does not matter," she replied. "Only what my father believes matters. He looks out for me."

Aeron grunted. "I had higher hopes for you, Valencia, having been watching you. One day, we shall escape Exile together. You are clever and pure-hearted. Exile cannot contain you."

"Do not try to trick me into partnering with you again."

"Trick? No tricks. You and I are not so different. We help each other to sell wood today, but one day, we shall partner and leave this place." He spat out the last word.

Valencia had never thought of leaving Exile without her father, and she had little hope he would ever reform. When prisoners entered Exile, soldiers placed arm bracelets around their biceps, which magically restrained them from leaving the town. The only way to escape was if her father demonstrated his repentance by performing a selfless deed. If he did that, his arm bracelet would fall off, and the two of them would be free to cross the border back into the general population—an unlikely event.

The thought of running away with this boy excited her. Despite a grating voice in her head that sounded like her father's, she turned the idea over slowly and carefully, as one might a shoat skewered on a spit. The image of her stepping outside of the boundaries of Exile with Aeron filled her heart with hope.

Aeron scratched his head. "Not today, but one day when we are both older, we will escape together. And once we are in the wide world, we shall bow and curtsey and dissolve the partnership. We shall live as neighbors, perhaps in Tusk or Bremen."

Valencia wanted more than anything to renounce the stance she had adopted and sell wood with this boy. He raised his eyebrows at her. "I am not my parents, Valencia, any more than you are your father."

"You are a rogue."

He grinned. "I do not deny it."

"And a charlatan."

"Guilty."

"And a bad person."

"Cutting, daughter of a criminal." Light and sarcastic, his tone endeared him to her. He turned away and began to accost the crowd, lecturing on the virtues of their wood. He peddled her goods without her permission, and again the two of them sold a pile of inventory though Valencia acted as if they weren't associated. Secretly, she was pleased her words hadn't made him leave.

At the end of the day, he hovered near as she counted their

pile of coins. He held out his hand. "And now, give me a majority of the money."

She gathered the metal pieces toward her chest. "Why?"

"Because you need to take home a little more but not too much. If you bring home what you have in your hands, your father will suspect you."

"We are not confederates. This was my wood."

He shrugged. "Then take the entire profit home. But if you listen to me, tomorrow you can take home one more coin. And the following week, one more, until, one day, you will bring home a pile of money and eat roasted chicken instead of gruel."

Valencia closed her eyes and breathed deeply. He was right, of course. His strategy would allow her to avoid the switch.

Aeron held out his hand and flexed his fingers, and Valencia gave him a majority of the coins. Aeron walked away but flipped a coin back to her. She placed the coin in her sock, the rest in her apron, and skipped home happily.

The days passed, and Valencia and Aeron's un-partnership flourished. She bettered her selling skills, but now she wouldn't think of turning away Aeron. She also learned another advantage of accepting her more-vocal partner. One particular day, Aeron offered to collect a second round of wood and left an improved Valencia to hawk their stock. As she called to pedestrians to inspect her merchandise, she gained the attention of two older boys, who surrounded her and threatened her for the day's profits. They stole the coins and ran away.

Aeron returned to find his partner curled up and rocking back and forth. He put his arms around her, and she cried on his shoulder. He whispered, "I will not leave you again. Not without someone here we trust looking after you. I promise."

In the days that passed, they talked about Exile, and Aeron taught her many things. He told her about King Shade and said his parents liked him, a sure sign the monarch was pure trouble. When the church bells chimed a certain rhythm, he explained they signified the death of an Exile resident. They rang once for each letter in the person's name, and if all bells tolled at the end, it meant the person repented before death. He talked about how convicts tried to tunnel out under Exile's boundaries but encountered an invisible wall.

One autumn day, Aeron looked up and examined the sky. "When we leave Exile, we will be free to go anywhere in Kingdom."

"Where would we go? And how would we eat?"

Aeron smiled. "Why do you think we are selling wood? We shall learn here and then venture forth, selling items we gather from nature."

Valencia's heart beat faster whenever he brought up the idea of escaping, but she never seriously thought of leaving Exile. She feared to abandon her father. When the time came to go, she would help Aeron but not escape herself. She liked Aeron, but she could endure her life here.

They worked together through the winter. Aeron bought Valencia a new woolen shirt with the money he had saved. It sheltered her from the cold winds, and she wore it under her ragged tunic so her father wouldn't see it. When the Reckoning came, the time of the year when the dead rose from their graves, Aeron walked her home before dark. People joked the two loved each other, but they maintained they were only friends.

Their arrangement continued into the summer of the next year, when one day Aeron didn't show up to work. Concerned but not overly worried, Valencia had developed her skills at bartering her items. Their merchandise now included oil and matches in addition to wood, the two of them having learned to trade some of their excess profits for other inventory.

The next day, Aeron appeared at noon, and Valencia noticed a faraway look in his eyes. He approached their barrels and stopped, staring forward as if lost. Valencia bit her lower lip. "Where have you been?"

Aeron turned his head and squinted as if trying to remember her. His lapse of memory lasted only for a moment, and then he smiled broadly. "I have found the girl of my dreams," he declared.

Valencia grabbed his arms. "How wonderful! Is she a child trapped here too?"

A gust blew his bangs away from his eyes. "I did not think to ask. It does not matter. She has lush, brown hair that extends to her waist. It is curly and tangled and it flies around her head when the wind blows. The ends of her hair are black as night. She is funny and demure and kind and interesting."

Valencia regarded him patiently. "All that at once? You spent the day yesterday with her?"

"I was on my way here, and she needed help carrying... something. I do not remember exactly what. Her arms are fragile. She and I walked around Exile all day, talking and staring into each other's eyes."

"I never thought of you as romantic. This girl must be something special."

"You do not know how special she is," said Aeron. "And here is the best part. We are going to leave Exile together. We shall find a small cottage—she calls it a little love nest—and live off of the produce of the land. I will become a farmer."

His new plan for leaving Exile piqued Valencia's curiosity. "A farmer? I thought you wanted to be a merchant."

"A merchant? That was before. I will be a farmer and provide for her. We shall be the happiest of people."

With his response, Valencia had one of her peculiar flashes of insight. In the past, the peddler girl had sensed the outcome of an event, good or bad, before making a decision. She had talked to Aeron about it, and he had thought her special perceptions only a hunch—but she knew the difference between her ability and a guess. Intuition often protected her in times of trouble, but the sensation of something being right or wrong before danger appeared came only rarely. The feeling that had overcome her now made her nervous about Aeron's infatuation, but Valencia didn't say a word.

Aeron sold their wood, though his usual energy flagged. Valencia herself did a better job of attracting customers. At the end of the day, Aeron took stock of the leftover inventory as he passed their earnings to his partner. "It seems I did not do well," he admitted.

"You are distracted."

He didn't respond. His attention focused on the end of the street.

Valencia examined their meager profits. "You were thinking of her, were you not?"

He crossed his arms. "Perhaps. 'Tis not a crime. Lovers often think of each other."

Again, Valencia sensed Aeron's behavior was off-kilter. She debated whether to confront him now, but refrained. "What are you waiting for? Go to her, you fool."

Aeron laughed and ran away. He didn't say good-bye or look back, as if, once she dismissed him, she no longer existed. She sighed and lowered her shoulders for her journey to her father.

After working alone the next day, Valencia dragged herself home. Her profits were light and dinner would be scarce, but at least she had made enough for a meager meal. Midsummer approached, and the girl longed for a taste of fresh fruit. As she entered her house, she halted before her father who stood in the middle of the room, switch in hand.

Valencia had never told her father about her arrangement with Aeron after the first day. Most of their neighbors, no matter what they had done in the far past, favored her and kept her secret.

"What is wrong, Father?"

"Are you with the boy I told you to stay away from?"

Valencia closed her eyes. For a long time, she hadn't thought about his threat concerning Aeron, but now, caught in her deception, she knew she would have to pay for it. "He is not a criminal."

"You admit it?"

"Yes."

Her father's face hardened. "I did not know whether to believe the girl with long hair or not. I have never seen her before. I wanted to believe you."

Valencia's jaw set. "Was her hair brown with dark ends?"

"You have made an enemy, Valencia, but it is no matter," he said. "We need to take care of this business of disobedience."

Valencia turned toward the wall, awaiting her punishment.

With her wounds still stinging the next day, Valencia moved slowly while collecting wood and straw. When she arrived at her corner, she was surprised to find Aeron near the barrels. He stood like a statue, looking off into space, arms listlessly at his side. She called to him, but he didn't acknowledge her until she touched his shoulder, nearly shouting his name. "What is the matter with you?" she asked.

"Nothing. I have had many thoughts, Valencia. I used to think insignificant thoughts. Remember those? A merchant in Tusk? Bah! Now I look forward to my twenty-acre farm and our cottage of love. And... Valencia does something trouble you?"

Valencia wanted to cry. "My father punished me last night for associating with you."

For a moment, Aeron's eyes focused, and his face softened. "After all this time and the money you and I have made, it still matters?"

"All that matters is I disobeyed him. But I have more I need to tell you."

Aeron gave her his full attention.

"I think your sweetmate told him about us."

Aeron snorted dismissively. "She would not have revealed our secret. I have talked to her about you, but I am sure she would love you if she knew you. Why would she tell?"

"I do not know. What do you know about her? Why is she here? Have you met her family?"

Aeron leaned against the barrels. "What does it matter? My own parents are criminals."

Valencia eyed him reluctantly. "Do you not want to know

about her?"

"Of course, but I know the best parts."

Valencia said, "I wonder..."

"You wonder what? I hate it when you say that."

The girl stuck out her chin. "You never used to. You used to say my wondering was how you knew I had a great idea."

Lowering his chin, Aeron stared at her through his bangs. "What is your *great idea* this time?"

"Aeron, bring her here to meet me. Bring...What is her name?"

"'Tis...It is..."

Valencia's eyes widened. "You do not know it?"

"I have never thought to ask. Her name is of no consequence."

"Aeron, be careful. I do not trust her. Please, as a friend, I beg you to listen to me."

Aeron leaned away from Valencia. "You are jealous."

"I am not," said Valencia. "You are my friend, but my friend only."

He bobbed his head as if seeing Valencia in a new light. "You have secretly hoped to become my sweetmate. Is it not so?"

Valencia closed her eyes and paused for a moment. "You know it is not true. We are confederates, but more importantly, we are friends."

"You are not my friend any longer." Aeron stepped away from her. "You are a jealous little girl with small dreams. Stay away from me, and stay away from her!"

Valencia's mouth dropped open. "I have done nothing to hurt her. She is the one—"

"Farewell, Valencia."

Valencia called after him, but he ignored her, disappearing into the crowd.

◆ ◆ ◆

The drenching rain appeared an hour later, and when it let

up, a light mist hung in the air all the rest of the day. Valencia found keeping the timber dry difficult, and so she borrowed a cloth from the barber. Even with her merchandise protected, she didn't sell many of her wares in the morning as the suffocating humidity soured people from purchasing moist wood. As she stood on the corner, begging people to buy straw, a scene unfolded before her, interrupting her in mid-sentence.

Aeron strolled across the center square arm in arm with a girl. His companion had flowing brown locks, a hawkish nose, and nearly nonexistent lips. They walked with their heads held high as if they were the king and queen leading a parade. They advanced in a straight line, unwavering, steps evenly measured. Neither acknowledged the wood peddler but moved slowly as she stared at them, mouth agape.

After the two disappeared into the mist, Valencia reflected on the scene and realized their promenade was a show solely for her benefit, likely the *girl's* idea. She wanted to run after them and shake Aeron out of his stupor.

The couple appeared again a few hours later. For a second time, they marched in the other direction, huddled together. Aeron's eyes never wavered but remained locked straight ahead, not acknowledging anyone, as he nearly ran into people. The girl walked alongside him, guiding him, then turned and glanced at Valencia. Aeron's companion's piercing, beady eyes winked at her.

Valencia nearly abandoned her post. She thought about her father and the punishment she had received the previous night. She must leave Aeron alone. Her former friend didn't want her anyway, had left in a huff, but his behavior bothered her. None of this made any sense, and Aeron now acted like a different person.

"I wonder."

The pair reappeared an hour before Valencia's normal time to pack up and go home. Again, they marched through the street in front of her. Aeron moved like the girl's puppet, seeming to be less aware of his surroundings each time they passed. If Valencia hadn't known him, she would have sworn he was blind. His partner guided his every step.

As the couple went by, the girl whispered to Aeron. He shook his head in response as they moved on. His companion turned toward Valencia and grinned wickedly, and then the mist swallowed them up again. This time Valencia decided to follow.

She packed her straw, her wood, her small pieces of parchment, her matches, and her twine into a bundle and started off through the mist after the two. At first, she thought she'd lost them but then arrived at an intersection leading off in three directions. Quietly, she closed her eyes.

She had to trust something, and she decided to trust her special feeling. She had never called it to her service before, and when it responded at this time, the impulse surprised her. The lucky intuition pointed Valencia to the middle lane, and she sped off in that direction. She ran past people, pushing them aside. Her blood coursed through her veins; the presentiment intensified.

The feeling showed Valencia the way and urged her onward. She worried not about herself but Aeron. Something was wrong, and she felt certain he was in danger.

Valencia ran into a dark alleyway and halted, convinced the two had entered here. Residents had littered the passage, a typical twisting and narrow alley, with trash and dangerous detritus strewn about. She hesitated, picking up a stick close at hand while wondering what awaited at the end of it. Convinced Aeron's girlfriend practiced sorcery, Valencia, a waif, possessed no defense against evil magic. As she hesitated, a cry cut across the night. Aeron!

Valencia sprinted down the alleyway and left whatever light from the street behind. As she hurried, she wrapped a paper around the stick in her hand and fumbled with a match. Before she lit it, a woman's voice, not a girl's, rasped a warning. "No farther!"

Valencia let her eyes adjust to the darkness and gasped at the scene in front of her. Aeron knelt, hunched over, arms around his waist, clearly wounded. His companion, no longer human, stood before him. Her hair had expanded, becoming large wings with downy plumage on the front. Her head had transformed into the head of a bird with a razor-sharp beak, and pointed face. She retained only her own beady eyes and her own stubby legs.

The bird squawked. "You dare to interrupt my supper?"

"Let him go!"

The thing's head shifted quickly in the spasmodic fashion typical of creatures of the air. She turned her attention to Aeron and then to Valencia. The way she moved made Valencia's skin crawl.

"If he wishes it..."

Aeron lifted his head, the light of reason restored to his eyes. Surely, he had only to run to Valencia and they could escape. Valencia gestured to him. "Come to me!"

He began to rise, but the girl sang, and Valencia stiffened at the tune. Her adversary emitted a haunting avian call, and Valencia found herself wanting to submit to the repulsive creature. The pitiable fowl only wanted love and acceptance, nothing more. The singer desired someone to be with, someone to give it protection. She was a defenseless little bird, alone in a large, cruel world.

Valencia shut her eyes and cleared her head. Aeron's eyes clouded yet again, and he drooped his head.

The bird's attention jerked toward Valencia. "You see? He is mine!"

"No!"

Valencia struck the match, but the monstrosity moved quickly. She reared back and screeched, and Valencia's breath stopped in her chest. The cry caused pain to Valencia, and no doubt to all who heard it. The shriek pulsated through the woodseller's brain like a spike to the head. Being nearer to the creature and weakened, Aeron groaned and trembled.

Valencia fumbled with her matches to light the stick. Aeron cried out, a plea of helplessness, and his eyes rolled upward. The supernatural wail had drained him, and the bird puffed itself up as Aeron withered.

Valencia lit the paper, and the fire spread to the stick, providing light. But she saw, to her dismay, she was too late. Depleted of energy, Aeron fell forward clumsily onto the lane.

The creature squealed a howl of triumph. She spread her wings to their full length, the tips of them touching the opposite alleyway walls. She ran toward Valencia on her human legs, ready to ascend. Then the fiend jumped and caught the air, and Valencia ducked to avoid the fowl's pummeling charge. The peddler girl realized at that moment she couldn't save Aeron, but she could honor their friendship and stop this beast from harming others.

She thrust her makeshift torch upward as the siren passed overhead. The fire caught on one of the miscreant's wings as it flew above Valencia. The monster warbled an astonished cry and veered, slamming into a wall while attempting to put out the fire with her other wing. She fell to the ground on her shoulder.

Valencia ran toward her enemy, her torch before her. The flame had nearly extinguished but that didn't deter the determined girl. Valencia thrust the torch at it again, catching the other wing on fire.

The monster screamed and tried to scramble away, but her efforts came too late. The fire had already caught and spread. The peddler girl knew the bird-woman would try to make it to the sea on the south side of town as she took off from the ground once again. Valencia watched the winged temptress as she shrieked repeatedly while she flew through the sky. Suddenly, the creature seemed to lose its sense of direction and spiraled to the ground, striking stone with a bone-crunching splat. A crowd gathered around it as it lay there, immobile.

Valencia turned and ran back to Aeron. She sat down next to him, holding his head on her lap and sobbing a steady stream of tears. His normally ruddy countenance was pale, his bangs hung over his eyes, and his chest no longer rose and fell.

When Valencia emerged from the alley, everyone stared at the torch in her hand. Gasps of astonishment followed, and she could almost read their minds. How had a young girl defeated such a powerful living thing? She shook her head and pointed down the alley. "There lies Aeron, son of a murderer and a thief. He caught the creature on fire with this flame before she murdered him."

The mob immediately accepted the answer, and a few people raced down to retrieve Aeron's body. Valencia slipped away as the crowd started to fashion their own stories of what had happened.

The very next day, Valencia stood and sold her wares again at the corner. The rain had returned and soaked her ragged clothes, her hair, and her stock. Her unfocused eyes didn't take in the throng shuffling before her, and she didn't care if people bought from her or not. She reflected briefly on how brave she had been the day before, nearly heroic, but none of her efforts had saved her friend. She had failed him, and deserved, like the rest of them, her Exile home.

The church bells broke into her reflections. Five rings sounded out, one for each letter of Aeron's name. She tilted her head to listen to the chimes as her tears mixed with raindrops. At the end of their tolling, the bells rang merrily, indicating another soul had escaped Exile.

FaerieForest

GOOSEBERRIES

Planet Constellation stormed into her home and threw a rock at the wall, missing her mother's right wing by only inches. Her own wings flashed, and her blue aura faded in the growing dusk. Flushed, she clenched her fists and drifted to a nearby chair made of the elephant-gray stem of a yucca plant.

Her mother put a hand on her chest, aura pulsing with alarm. "Goodness, Planet! What is this all about?"

"I did not get it, Ma. The diplomacy council rejected me. The only ones who will take me are the gooseberry bunch."

Her mother pointed to another stool across the room, a four-legged piece of furniture woven together from grapevines. The wooden seat skidded on its own to Planet's mother, and she floated to it, crossing her legs and hovering inches above its surface. "Looking for gooseberries is an honorable job for a pixie, Planet."

Planet looked at her mother through her chocolate-colored bangs. "You do not need magic for diplomacy. I am good with people. I have elven friends. Why did they turn me down?"

Her mother placed her hand on Planet's leg. "You need magic when negotiations do not go well. Sometimes pixies must resort to magic to escape...or defend."

"I can defend myself." Planet crossed her arms. "My fizz spell improves daily. And I will not need to escape or fight. I am an exceptional talker. Ask any of my teachers!"

"They did not mean it as a compliment," replied her mother. "Negotiations are not always successful. Think of the way humans treat us."

The young pixie shivered but didn't respond. Some humans were kind, but the scalpers made leaving their communities treacherous for fairies.

"Planet, gooseberry expeditions are fun. You will travel over the Faerie Forest looking for the one ingredient that enhances all magic, the gooseberry. Finding one will make you the envy of the forest."

"It should, considering no one has ever found one."

Her mother used her right wing to point at a portrait hanging on their wall of a pixie with his chest puffed out. "Not true. Do not forget Trillum. He searched the Forest of Death and found a blooming gooseberry bush. Since then, his honorable name has been well known throughout all of Kingdom."

"Trillum, Trillum, Trillum." Planet turned away and pulled her arms tighter around her body. "We have all heard of him. He lived ages ago. Who has found a gooseberry bush in your lifetime? Do you know of anyone?"

"I know if you find one, our family will be the pride of Faerie Forest."

Planet looked sideways at her mother. "We would, would we not?"

Her mother nodded.

"Was not Uncle Orion also a gooseberry explorer?" asked Planet.

"No. Your uncle was a prospector. He should never have

gone to the Den of Scorpus."

Planet peered at the picture of Trillum. "Have we ever had a gooseberry explorer in the Constellation family as far as you can remember?"

Her mother's eyes glazed over and her wings drooped slightly. "I do not recall anyone."

Planet herself recollected a gooseberry patrol floating through the rain while the rest of the community celebrated a holiday. "Ma, we both know the best pixies in school do not become gooseberry explorers. The job is often reserved for those at the bottom...like me."

Planet's mother tilted her head. "Work hard, my daughter, and find a gooseberry. I know how you feel about Celeste. Your sister has garnered many accolades."

Planet sniffed. "I think she stole all the magic when she was born, leaving me with nothing."

"What a silly thought, dear one," replied her mother. "We all have different gifts we bring to the forest. For example, you are exuberant and daring while Celeste is more reserved and cautious. Your sister could never be a gooseberry explorer."

Planet lifted her chin. "True. I suppose she could not."

"You are uniquely fitted to this role. Do not underestimate its importance to the pixies or Kingdom."

Reflecting on her mother's words, Planet glowed a brighter blue.

Planet scoured the floor of Faerie Forest, allowing her aura to light the nooks and crannies hidden by the trees. The patrol searched in an uninhabited section of the woods where no pixie houses were tucked, like nests, in the tree limbs. The trees, large in a pixie frame of reference but only slightly taller than an adult human being, consisted of maples growing apples, pines running wine as sap, and oak trees whose scent was of the sea.

The fairies floated through the woods like will-o-the-wisps with a purpose. As she flew along, Planet illuminated the emerald grass with a whale-blue color. She spotted a wayward berry and her aura turned a deeper shade, but when she identified it as a boysenberry, she moved on. The lead fairy, wearing a golden cap and a necklace made of barbs, signaled a break, and Planet sat on the path with a sigh, massaging her wings.

The young pixie made out a fellow pixie floating toward her—his aura a murky green, the shade of moss in shadows. She recognized his color immediately. He landed as she greeted him. "Hi, Compactor."

"Aye, Planet. Searching for gooseberries?"

She stretched her back, and her bones twanged like banjo strings. "I am going to be the first to find one."

"Why you?"

"Because that is my destiny." Her eyes flashed.

"Last week, you told me you would run away if the only choice offered was gooseberry explorer," he said.

Planet scratched the top of her head. "I thought it was a low job. Remember how we used to shine our lights in the faces of workers on gooseberry patrol? We were wrong. I used to think only unskilled pixies were explorers, but they are not. I am proud to be one. Why yesterday—"

Compactor interrupted her. "You think you are going to be the first one to find a gooseberry?"

"After Trillum, yes. I have a wonderful idea. Why not join us?"

Compactor nodded toward a nearby field. "My job is Faerie Forest's groundskeeper."

Planet grabbed his arm, excited by her idea. "Let the ground take care of itself, as it has for eons. Let us hunt gooseberries together."

Compactor stared off into the distance. "I am not interested in searching for something no one has ever seen."

"And why not?"

"I had an aunt once on gooseberry patrol. She spent her whole life scouring the forest up and down, covering every path, every tree, but never found a gooseberry. By the end of her life, she had accomplished nothing."

"You are a Negative Nilly. Why are we friends again?"

"I am a good listener."

A whistle cut through the air. "My signal," Planet told him. "I am off to find a gooseberry. Remember, when I find it, you can say you knew me when. I will live in the Grand Oak, and I will wave down to you and the rest of the peasants as you go by."

Compactor smirked at her teasing, then Planet flew away and started her search again. Before she left him too far behind, however, she turned around to wave, but saw he didn't even notice the gesture. He sat with his arms on his knees, staring solemnly at his hands.

At the end of her shift, Planet entered her home, stumbling over a stool near the doorway. Her mother, at her easel painting a portrait, observed her child wide eyed. "You were out late, Planet."

"What is father cooking tonight?"

"Celeste is cooking," replied her mother. "She has a new spell to try out."

"She is a *horrible* cook."

"Top of her class."

Her blue daughter snorted. To Planet, Celeste's fairy mush tasted like the sole of a boot. Recently, Celeste had invited a few elders over to show off her skill in culinary incantations. While everyone else fawned over her sister's exquisite, magical seasoning, Planet faked gagging on it. She and Compactor had broken out in laughter during Celeste's formal dinner party.

Now the newly employed pixie flew to her square room and threw herself onto the bed, exhausted. Her mother fluttered in after her. "Why were you out late, Planet?" she asked.

Planet rolled over onto her side. "After everyone went home, I put in extra hours looking for gooseberries."

Her mother lowered herself to the ground, her wings carefully draped behind her back. "Maybe in the future you should come home on time."

"Why? If I am going to be the person to find it, I had better give it my all."

"Planet, you should temper your enthusiasm with recreation. We pixies excel at play and pranks. Remember our saying, 'To play is to polish one's light.'"

Planet lit up the room with her stunning aura. "Still shining, Ma. Remember what you told me. I will be the first to find one in centuries. Nothing will stop me."

"My dear, please be patient. Do not spend all your time on your job." Her mother left the room, wringing her hands.

Without another thought, Planet rolled over and fell asleep.

Planet's troop made its way back to her neck of the forest after a three-day excursion in a swale, searching among the twisted vines of Hangman's Fortune. Regrettably, no one had found a gooseberry, not surprising in a part of the forest where little fruit grew—but Planet was not discouraged. Moreover, her absence meant Celeste had to look after more chores at home. Planet grinned wickedly at the thought of her sister picking up Tardalong waste in their backyard.

Served her right, as most often Planet had to do the work around the house while Celeste practiced her advanced magic unceasingly. True, unlike her sister, magic came naturally to Planet. She hardly ever studied. Why practice like her booooooring sister when so many exciting adventures beckoned her outside? She, Compactor, Rayshine, and their elven friends played "Trip the Troll" nearly every night.

They were an hour away from her neighborhood when the captain whistled a break. Planet decided to sit with a friendly, elderly male pixie named Bali. He smacked his lips as he bit into a red, edible toadstool. Planet liked Bali and talked to him non-stop when they worked together. Bali, hard of hearing, would smile at her and nod as she rambled on. With her loquacity and his deafness, they made good companions.

His hearing was better today as he greeted Planet. "Have you found any gooseberries, young lady?"

"No, but I will." Planet's aura brightened at the thought.

"That's the spirit. This is my last day as an explorer. My wife, Wilifred, and I have grand plans."

Planet nodded sorrowfully. Bali had spent all of his life looking for a gooseberry but had never found one. The pixie girl leaned toward him. "I will miss your old way of speaking, the way you run words together. No one says *that's* any more, Bali. They say *that is*."

"You should try speaking the old way. You'd love it."

Planet smiled. His attempt to get her to speak the old way was as hopeless as his attempts to find gooseberries.

Bali tilted his head. "You're sad I've spent my entire life looking for a gooseberry but never found one, aren't you?"

"I never said so."

Bali sighed and looked at her patiently. "Ah, the innocence of our newest members. Planet, could you find no other position than searching for gooseberries?"

Planet's blue aura faded a little. "This is the only job they would let me do."

Bali bit a piece of the toadstool, chewed a moment, and swallowed it. "I see you've been spending extra time searching for the magical fruit?"

Planet floated above the ground, uplifted by a sudden shift in mood. "I thought I found one the other day, but it turned out to be a Yowler's pupa. I was quite embarrassed. I shall not make that mistake again—"

"Planet, please listen to me," said Bali. "I favor you, so I will tell you something you won't want to hear, but it's best you know. Your parents should tell you this, but if they won't, then I will."

Planet settled herself back on the ground. She sensed she really wouldn't like what he wanted to tell her, but she had to know. "I'm listening."

"No such thing as a gooseberry exists."

Planet blinked. "What?"

Bali's eyes lowered. He wouldn't meet her gaze, as if regretting revealing the secret. "It's a fabrication."

"You are wrong." Planet's nostrils flared. "That makes no sense."

"It does. Some pixies aren't as gifted as others. They struggle with spell wielding and most of the mystical arts. They can't do the usual work required of our kind. Yet they must busy themselves with some task or other. The elders created the gooseberry legend to give them something to do while other pixies perform the real work."

"But...you have spent your entire life looking for gooseberries!"

Wearily, Bali lifted his head. "I've spent my entire life keeping out of the way of the rest of our clans while they have protected, nourished, and entertained me. From that perspective, gooseberry patrol is not a bad career. I have no pretensions I do anything useful."

Planet stood. "Bali, gooseberries must exist. They must!"

"Most pixies know gooseberries don't exist. As they grow up and become productive members of society, they learn that gooseberry hunting is a lie. A nothing occupation."

Planet shook her head. "It cannot be."

And yet, Planet knew. She knew.

"Planet?"

"Go away."

"Planet, I am your best friend."

"You are a liar. Why did you not tell me?"

Compactor joined Planet in the secret grove the two of

them shared. Planet's arms were wrapped around her legs. She brushed the tears from her face.

The green pixie bit his lip. "Is this about gooseberries?"

"I suppose you enjoyed your little joke on me. You and all the rest. Poor, stupid Planet. Let us send her on a wild gooseberry chase."

"You have it wrong, Planet. Whoever told you will be in trouble if the Faerie Council finds out. Penalties are imposed for telling."

Planet swallowed hard while fresh tears fell from her eyes. "Penalties? Who cares? I worked hard looking for something that does not exist!"

"You were excited. You were going to change the world," said Compactor in his gentlest voice.

Planet buried her face in her hands. "The world is better off without me."

"Come with me, Planet. Perhaps I can find you a job as a groundskeeper."

"I do not need your help," she snapped. "I may continue to look for gooseberries. After all, are we sure they do not exist?"

"Planet, think of the name. Who would name a berry after a goose?"

He was right. How could she be so blind to the truth? Dumb, idiotic Planet!

Compactor said, "Perhaps you can quit and take care of your parents? The Faerie Council will not force you to remain on gooseberry patrol. Your job will be to stay out of the way."

Planet sniffed. "You mean, stay out of the way of the more important pixies, like you?"

Compactor shrank into himself. "You have twisted my meaning. You are my best friend."

Planet hugged her knees closer. "I cannot face them, and I will not continue doing this."

"They may banish you if you do not comply."

"I will not let them banish me." Planet stood and wiped her eyes. She squared her shoulders and looked hard at Compactor. "I have thought of another plan."

"Groundskeeper? With me?"

Planet shook her head. "They will not let me, Compactor, and you know it. No, I will leave Faerie Forest. I will run away."

"Mingle with the humans? Are you mad?" asked the green pixie.

Planet twisted the hem of her tunic. "At first, my family will not notice. When they do, I will be on my way. I will have adventures, Compactor. Adventures no other fairy ever had."

"You will be killed."

Planet lifted her chin. "I can take care of myself."

"Planet, do not do this."

Planet looked south where Faerie Forest ended and the woods of Kingdom began. "I must, Compactor. This is the end of my life here. I will not be renowned like Trillum, but I will make my way in the world."

"Planet..."

She took his hands. "Good-bye, Compactor. You have been a loyal friend."

He opened his mouth to try to stop her, but she zipped away. She flew like a blue streak, zig-zagging through the forest, leaving him and her family behind.

The innkeeper who had caught Planet trying to steal a glass of sweetwater crossed her arms and examined the dishes she had made the pixie wash. She swiped a gloved finger along a pan, held the digit up to her eyes and observed the result, her mouth curling downward. Human-sized, Planet slumped over the stool she had been standing on for the past two hours while scraping bits of food from plates. The pixie cocked an ear when a distant church bell rang twice, signaling two hours after midnight.

Planet pouted. "You promised me food and drink if I cleaned all the dishes."

"When was the last time you ate?" the innkeeper asked.

The pixie's stomach rumbled if on cue. "Two days ago."

The human woman, brown tresses rolling down her back, looked about twenty years old. At Planet's response, her features softened, and she exited the room, returning seconds later with a platter holding a hunk of bread, two slices of cheese, and a mug of wine. The innkeeper set this down in front of the famished dishwasher.

Planet grabbed the bread, broke off a large piece, and stuffed it into her mouth. She lifted the mug to her lips.

"Slow down," advised the proprietress. She leaned against the wall. "You will get indigestion if you eat too quickly."

Planet eyed her, but followed her instructions, chewing the bread with relish. Though the crust was a bit stale, the bread's soft interior tasted of melted butter, and the savory food sparked her weary senses. Planet added a slice of cheese for her second bite.

The innkeeper placed her clenched hands on her hips. "Now tell me what a pixie is doing in this part of Kingdom?"

Planet spoke with her mouth full. "I uhm no puhxie."

"I saw your shadow through the doorway," replied her companion. "The shape of the wings could only belong to a pixie." She held up her hand. "Relax. I shut the door to keep your secret."

Planet chewed slowly and eyed the room. The fairy carefully observed the woman standing in front of the exit. A fizz spell aimed at her face might disable her long enough to run away.

The innkeeper noticed her shift of attention. "I told you not to worry. I would never hand a pixie to a scalper. 'Tis an odious and wretched act."

Planet wanted to make a bold statement but worried that her voice would tremble. She pushed away harrowing memories of her journey from Faerie Forest across the farmlands of Kingdom. Hiding beneath a lily pad in a marshy pond while scalpers beat the bushes to find her, leaping out of the path of a pack of centaurs, and awakening under a giant wasp were encounters that only began to describe Planet's ordeals. Most people she'd met had been cruel, with the exception of a band of elves she'd encountered at Soro's Well. They had provided the pixie with sustenance so she would have enough energy to seek shelter at the inn.

Instead of saying something profound, Planet spoke her mind without forethought. "I can defend myself against scalpers. Top of my class, I was."

The woman across from her turned down one side of her mouth. "Well, Top-Of-Your-Class, do you have a name and a reason for why you are so far from home?"

"I am Planet," Planet blurted out and grimaced. She knew better than to tell a stranger her real name.

Her companion dropped her arms to her side. "Your name is safe with me too."

"And I am here to find a...gooseberry. People say they do not exist, but I want to make sure and travel around Kingdom. Many odd and interesting artifacts may be found with a little effort."

"Indeed, many magical items do exist," the human answered. "But gooseberries do not exist in Kingdom. I suspect you already know that."

Planet kicked the bottom of her shoe against the stool's leg. "Yes, I learned it recently. I suppose they are not real."

The woman grinned. "I did not say they were not real, but I would advise you to abandon your quest. I have a better offer."

The fairy blinked. "Offer?"

"A job." The woman put her hand on Planet's shoulder, a gentle gesture of support. "How would you like to meet peculiar people and hear their wild tales? You could do that here at the Inn of Five."

Recognizing the benign intention behind the proposal, Planet sat up straighter on the stool, her wings emerging. "I would like that."

"Good. I need a new barmaid. My name is Penta, Ms. Planet. 'Tis good to meet you."

Planet placed her hand on top of Penta's gloved one and

thought about this opportunity. From here, listening to the inn's patrons and their stories, she could learn about Kingdom and all it had to offer. And when she decided to leave, whether Kingdom was ready or not, she would hold her head high and embark on a grand adventure.

ROSE AND COAL

Rose Schell jumped when the front door of her farmhouse crashed open and Coal Whisper, shoeless and pallid, stumbled inside. Rose reached for Coal and steadied her, understanding at once the reason for the girl's abrupt entrance. Apparently, her domestic situation had turned so dire this time that Coal had run away and left her slippers behind. Rose looked down and gasped. Kingdom's uneven paths and root-entangled trails had turned Coal's feet ugly shades of black and blue. The farm girl threw her arms around her bruised best friend. "Again?" she whispered.

Coal nodded and started crying. Rose surmised the pain of running three miles without shoes was nothing compared to the hurt inside. She escorted Coal to a worn-out divan with goose-feather cushions, helped her take a seat, and crouched down before her. Rose rubbed Coal's feet with a gentle touch. "Why this time?"

"She had no reason."

Rose shook her black curls at the answer. At fourteen years old, she believed everything happened for a reason. "There must be some explanation, Coal."

"I was washing the floor when she stormed in," Coal replied. "She was angry about something. You have seen her moods."

Rose's brows furrowed. Oh yes, she had seen Madame Whisper in one of her spells, and Rose had held back her own rage for the sake of her friend.

A tear rolled down Coal's dirty yet pale cheeks. "I did not say anything after she hit me. At first, I thought I had missed a spot, but she focused on me, not the chore. She hit the back of my head, and I lay there, not daring to move."

"'Tis like you, Coal, to take punishment without responding." Rose continued to massage her friend's ankles.

The other girl hitched her breath. "No one crosses you, Rose. Anyway, my mother grabbed my head and pulled it back. Then she lifted me by cupping her hand under my chin. Her eyes terrified me."

Rose put her hand tenderly on Coal's arm.

Coal rubbed her straight, black tresses in thought. "She had torture in her eyes, but she released me. I ran."

"And you came straight here?"

"Where else?"

"You will stay here. My parents will be glad to have you again. Do you want my father to talk to her?"

Rose's companion huddled in on herself. "No! Remember the last time they spoke?"

Rose hadn't seen her friend for days. Coal's mother had locked her away to starve. The incident had taught them that Rose's parents could shelter Coal for a short time but not protect her indefinitely.

Rose hugged Coal, then stood. "Rest. You are safe now. I am making stew. Then we shall eat and talk. We will find a way to restore sense to your mother."

Coal's eyes glazed over. "Oh, she was a noblewoman. I admired her when I was a small child."

Rose attended to the supper as Coal leaned back on the divan. The curly-headed girl cut carrots with her dull knife and threw them into the pot. She needed water from their well, though didn't want to leave Coal even for a minute. But noticing her dark-haired friend had her eyes closed, praying, she picked up her pail.

Rose left her cottage and escaped into the pastoral world she knew and loved. She was a farmer's daughter, a loyal subject of the world of Kingdom—a world of fairies and monsters, of kings and queens.

On her way to the well, Rose reflected on how Madame Faye Whisper's comportment toward her daughter continued to deteriorate. When she and Coal had met as children, Faye, while never a warm person, took care of her daughter. A rich woman with sharp features, Coal's mother had changed for the worse the past two years. Her smile, no longer patient and mirthful, had turned conniving as if she was planning some wicked scheme.

Rose drew water from the well, pondering Coal's plight when a thought struck her. Perhaps they had no way to change Madame Whisper's mind or her behavior. If that was true, Coal's only option was to run away. Rose thought for a moment of sheltering her friend but knew that Coal couldn't live with her. Faye Whisper, even if she was cruel to her daughter, wanted her at home. Rose figured Coal's mother kept her daughter close to demand a costly dowry for her best friend's meekness and beauty.

Coal would have to leave another way.

Rose wanted to talk to the third companion in their circle of friends, Lolander Fyrekilm. If Lol were here, he would know just what to do. Broad-shouldered and bulky, Lol was gentle and light on his feet and an excellent listener. The three trusted and looked after each other and laughed the most when all three were together. Lol admired Coal and would do anything for her.

Rose reflected on her two best friends and snorted, picturing little, gentle Coal and square-framed, hairy Lol: one, a lumbering tree of a boy; the other, a budding flower of a girl. Rose pictured a garden with only Lol's tree and Coal's flower and saw how beautiful they were together.

Rose stopped in her tracks as an idea to solve her best friend's troubles formed in her mind. Lol could marry Coal.

◆ ◆ ◆

Rose distracted Coal by asking her to help with dinner, and the young maiden with the dark tresses busied herself cutting up more vegetables. Coal wiped her eyes as she labored, but she was a hard worker. She cut the eyes off a potato, careful to remove as little skin as possible. As everyone in Kingdom knew, potato eyes in stew brought the worst sort of luck.

When Rose's parents arrived home, they greeted Coal with embraces and kisses on her cheeks. Coal told her story, and Rose's parents sympathized and offered their home, but Rose knew her friend wouldn't stay long. They all sat down as a family and shared their meal. Afterward, Rose asked Coal to join her in a walk around the farm to ward off Tardalongs, hairy beasts of the forest. Rose fetched her bow, and the two left, holding hands. They walked in the gathering darkness, looking for any sort of vermin daring to cross the farm's boundaries. Rose hummed a tune while Coal peered into the distance.

"Lol said he would drop by tomorrow morning," Rose remarked.

Coal released Rose's hand and clapped her hands together. "How wonderful! I have not seen him in a long time."

Rose inclined her head, pleased to hear Coal's remark. "I am sure he feels the same way as well. This will spare him the trip to your house."

Coal put a hand on her chest. "My house? He never comes to my house."

Rose said, "Yes, he was adamant about seeing you. His wish to do so is, of course, natural."

"What is natural?"

"Dear Coal." Rose tsked. "You must have noticed."

Coal blinked twice rapidly. "Noticed?"

"The way he looks at you. 'Tis as if he is looking toward heaven's gates," said Rose.

Coal halted while Rose continued on without looking back. Her friend gasped. "You jest."

"And why would I do that?"

"Because he favors *you*. I have seen his look of longing."

"You are mistaken," said Rose as Coal stepped alongside her. "You know as well as I that it is you who has won his heart."

Coal's giggle cut through the evening's silence. She concluded her mirth with a snort. "Not I!"

Rose tossed her hair backward. "Perhaps not. Why would he be attracted to the most beautiful maiden in the land?"

"You are very beautiful as well, Rose."

"A far cry from you, my dear. Do not deny it! The devil takes your tongue if you suggest you are not one of the most beautiful girls we know."

Color rose in Coal's cheeks. She did not reply but looked down as they began to walk again.

Rose carefully avoided a prairie dog's hole. "Beautiful, rich, eligible. Lol would be a fool not to notice you."

"I was so sure..." said Coal, mostly to herself. "But perhaps...?"

"He will be here tomorrow. I think the two of you should take a walk without me, and you will see what I already know." Rose smiled to herself at her successful planting of the idea.

Coal smiled and blushed all at once.

"I spot a fox a few yards off," observed Rose. "Let us be quick and scare him away."

Rose unstrapped her bow and hid a further grin from her friend. More than one clever animal stalked through this night.

❖ ❖ ❖

Rose lay in bed thinking about her fib to Coal, done for her friend's benefit—so was it really a lie? No, Lol would be a fool to ignore Coal. He would receive a dowry from Madame Whisper and betroth the prettiest girl for miles around. Rose, in comparison, was barely noticeable, even if she was the second-most eligible bachelorette in their part of Kingdom. Furthermore, Lol needed to rescue Coal from her mother. Rose was not, by any means, in peril.

True, Coal mentioned Lol was attracted to her, but her friend was quite naïve. Lol was no more interested in Rose than the stars were larger than the sun. Rose was poor, she was plain, she was headstrong. Lol would want a compliant sweetmate, not a hard egg like her.

Yet, she had to show him. Men were so ignorant about the ways of the heart; if left to themselves, they chose the wrong girl nine times out of ten. Lol would end up married to a female sprite without Rose's intervention. She needed to talk to him before Coal woke up the next morning. If Rose had a few moments alone with Lol, he would be courting Coal before midday tomorrow.

◆ ◆ ◆

Rose spotted the broad-shouldered form of Lol through the kitchen window while her friend Coal was busy sewing. Rose excused herself, ran across the muddy farmyard, and intercepted Lol. Greeting him, she took his arm and directed him away from her farmhouse.

"Where are we going?" asked Lol, eyes wide with excitement.

"To the orchard. I want to tell you a secret."

Lol grinned bearishly. "A secret? I have one too. I came to talk to you about it."

Rose stopped at the edge of the sweet-smelling grove of fruit trees. Standing against a pear tree, she held up her hand. "I will go first. Lol, we have been friends for four years. Ever since Coal and I saved you from that dwarf."

Lol's eyes dropped to Rose's calloused fingers, evidence of all of the practicing she put in with her bow. Playfully, he put his palm to hers. "You did not save me. I was at a disadvantage and needed time."

Rose wrinkled her brow. "Anyway, I wanted to let you know Coal slept here last night." She turned to him and stopped. "Is that not wonderful news?"

Lol dropped his hand, and he squinted at Rose. "I enjoy Coal's company," he agreed in a mild tone.

Rose put her hands on her hips in indignation. "Lolander Fyrekilm! Are you telling me this is ordinary news?"

"Begging your pardon, but Coal seems to be at your house more than she is at her own."

Rose took his arm again, and Lol looked down. She led him through the orchard, which was bursting with ripe apples, plums, pears, and olives. The fragrance of each tree mixed with the next pungently and pleasingly. Rose stroked a branch as she passed by. "Her mother treats her horribly. Perhaps one day a knight will come and woo her away."

Lol brushed an apple with his hairy knuckles. "'Tis a sweet ending for a worthy maiden," he said.

"She is beautiful. She is the most beautiful girl I have ever seen."

"Agreed."

"And she is the daughter of a rich farmer."

Lol gazed down at Rose's hand on his arm. "Coal is fortunate."

"The man who wins her heart shall be fortunate—not Coal. She has enough grace to be nobility. Who knows? If her farm has a few good seasons, she may enter the upper caste."

Lol laughed. "The next thing you will say is she will be queen."

Rose sucked in her breath. "Lol, you muttonhead. Have you not been listening to anything I have said?"

His eyes sparkled. "I have absorbed every word."

"Then why have you not figured out that you could be her knight? You could be the one for Coal."

Lol stepped back and rubbed his beard. "I am no knight.

You know this better than anyone."

Rose waved her hand. "You focus too much on the wrong things. What is a knight anyway? Chivalrous, kind, respectful. Are these not your own qualities, Lol?"

Lol ducked under a branch of a pear tree. "I thank you for thinking so highly of me. It is undeserved, I assure you. But I perceive an obstacle to your fantasy."

"And what is that?" Rose demanded.

Lol said, "The maiden does not favor me—an insurmountable problem."

Rose stopped and swung to face Lol. The six-foot, muscle-bound man with the tawny beard towered over the slight girl, yet she was the one in control. "How men do not pay attention. Her face lights up when she sees you. She becomes awkward and quiet, shy."

"This is Coal's nature," Lol observed.

"Not in this way. I am her best friend and wished I were her sister. I tell you that she favors you. How could she feel otherwise? You would lay your life down for her, would you not?"

"Of course, but—"

"Then listen to me," said Rose. "Whatever you may think, you are as smitten as she. You are never completely yourself in front of her."

"I am not?"

"Of course not. You are entirely taken with her. I see it in your eyes. They reveal the truth."

"Perhaps you misinterpret them." Lol blushed.

Rose put a hand on her hip. "Lol, listen to me. You and I are best friends."

"Absolutely."

"And you would trust me in this matter?"

Lol rocked back and forth. "Normally, yes. But I think—"

"Then trust me now. I have a strong feeling about you and Coal. She will make you a happy man." Rose's eyes pierced him. "No one will do better."

Lol asked, "You really think so?"

"With my whole heart."

Lol peered at the tips of his boots. "She is beautiful."

Rose took his arm again and led him out of the orchard. "You are a lucky man. The two of you favor each other. It is your destiny to be with her."

"But, what would I say?"

"Ask her name."

"Her name? I know her name. 'Tis Coal Whisper."

Rose stared at him through her curls. "Coal is the name her mother gave her. Her mother says she named Coal thus because her hair is black as coal, but I have my doubts. Coal has another name, her real name. Ask her. She will only tell you if she is attracted to you."

Rose knew Lol was a man of few words, and this duffer needed a little encouragement. Coal's nickname would be a good way to start the conversation. Once they started talking, the two would fall in love. They didn't know it yet, but they were perfect for each other.

Rose and Lol emerged from the cluster of pear trees, and Rose brushed back her curls. "I will return home. Wait here for a moment and make it look as if it was *your* idea to come for a visit."

Lol pouted. "It *was* my idea to come for a visit."

"It was not. I thought of your visit last night," Rose replied.

Lol blinked at her logic. Rose continued, "I will return first, and then you shall arrive five minutes later. I will make an excuse for you to talk to Coal alone."

Rose strode off, so absorbed in her own plans she had forgotten to ask Lol the reason why he had come to her farm.

When Lol arrived, Rose asked both what they thought of the king's current mistress, a universally despised woman. Lol's stuttering and unfinished sentences pained Rose to hear. Coal's responses weren't much better. She spoke an octave higher than her regular voice and giggled at everything Lol said. When he mentioned his dwarf friend had broken his leg, Coal erupted in a snicker ending in a snort. Rose wanted to put the cooking kettle over her own head in embarrassment.

Rose looked out the window. "Would the two of you travel through the orchard to collect water from the stream for dinner? Take the kettle. Lol can carry it back."

Coal looked puzzled. "What should I do?"

Rose wanted to cover her eyes in frustration. Scrambling for a reason, she said the first thing that came to her mind. "You always collect the sweetest water, dear Coal."

"Oh," chirped Coal. And then perhaps the realization dawned on her as to what Rose was trying to accomplish. "Oh," she said again, this time understanding. When Lol offered his arm, Coal looked at it in surprise, and then she said "Oh" a third time. She filled the third "oh" with sentiment and expectation.

The two left, and a grinning Rose watched them go. This was the beginning of a love story bards would sing about for years, and she would be able to say she had started it all. She was the one who had brought them together—the reason for their romance.

Rose's reverie faded when she had a horrible premonition. She pictured Lol leaning down too quickly to kiss Coal and smacking his head against hers. No, Lol would be gentle, would he not? Was he the one she should worry about? She thought of her friend standing with her back to the stream, lips pouted, shaking in anticipation. While waiting, her foot might slip and down she would go, into the water.

Rose shook her head. "I have to do everything."

They had disappeared into the orchard, and Rose left her farmhouse and ran after them. If Lol was clumsy or Coal acted like a ninny, she would have to interrupt them and set them right. First impressions were the most important.

Rose ran through the grove while dodging tree branches. As she came to the boundary of a line of pear trees, she spotted the two of them at the edge of a stream. She slid behind a tree after she saw them standing before each other, Lol's hands on Coal's arms.

Rose smiled to herself with her back to the tree and then peeked around the trunk. As Coal spoke, Lol seemed focused on her, taking in every word. He smiled and nodded in agreement with the winsome maiden. Rose was sure her friend had told him her name, and he approved. The awkwardness had passed, and the courting had begun.

Rose's plan was working! The two of them knew they were destined for each other, but still Rose couldn't help but feel something was amiss. They stood close to each other—good. They stared at each other with...what was that? Desire? She hoped so. So what was missing?

Lol leaned toward Coal, and Rose sucked in her breath. What was he doing? He was going to kiss her, but the timing was too soon! He had hardly courted her. Surely Coal, being a lady, would pull away. She would never let him kiss her.

But her friend surprised Rose. Coal tipped her head back and closed her eyes. A rush of unexpected irritation entered Rose's heart. How could Coal allow him to kiss her? They hardly knew each other. Untrue, but he was too forward, and she was too agreeable. He was going too fast!

She murmured, "This isn't right!"

Rose plucked a pear and watched as Lol moved toward Coal as slowly as an indecisive caterpillar. Rose was an excellent archer and her aim was true with more than arrows. She hurled the pear with as much force as she could muster. When the fruit struck Coal on the shoulder, the missile caused her to lose her footing, and she screamed and, indeed, as Rose had but a short while before foreseen, fell into the stream.

Rose ran to them as Lol entered the water and helped Coal out. When Rose arrived, a dripping-wet Coal stared at the fruit archer in surprise. "Did you throw it?"

Rose stopped before the two and looked back and forth. She pressed her lips together and nodded. "I did not know what I was doing, dear Coal."

Coal frowned and wiped her wet shoulder covered in pear

pulp and river water. She crossed her arms over her body. "I need to change my clothes. And to think, pear used to be my favorite fruit."

"I will help you." Rose offered her hand.

Coal refused her assistance. "I would rather you remain here and apologize to Lol."

Rose dropped her arm. "But I did not do anything to Lol."

Coal's eyes flashed. "Are you sure?"

Coal marched away, shoulders hunched, and Rose and Lol watched her leave. Lol set a hand on Rose's shoulder, gently turning her to face him. Rose stared blankly into his doe-brown eyes. "What does she mean?"

Lol's grip squeezed her shoulder. "Why did you throw the pear, Rose?"

"I thought...I thought you and Coal were going too fast." She humphed at him and lifted her chin. "Imagine, the two of you kissing so quickly. For shame."

"I thought I was her knight?"

Rose shuffled awkwardly. "Not very knightly."

"A knight should kiss his true love, should he not?"

Rose's brows creased. "Of course, but..."

"But she is not my true love, is she?"

Rose stiffened. "Of course she is. She is beautiful, charming, lovely. How could you not like her?"

Lol's eyes remained fixed on Rose. "Coal is all of those things, true. But perhaps my maiden should be stubborn and headstrong. Perhaps she should be less of a rich farmer's daughter and more of a matchmaker?"

Rose looked at her broad-shouldered friend sharply. She tried to say something, but couldn't find the words.

So Lol spoke instead. "Do you feel the same way as I do? You are more to me than simply a friend. I made up my mind to tell you when I came to visit until you led me astray. I...You...I..."

Rose's pear-launching arm was suddenly around his waist. The other arm, envying the first, followed suit, and Rose found herself fondly hugging the hirsute man. No, the problem wasn't that he had been moving too fast with Coal. When true love sparks, a kiss is imminent. Her brain caught up with what her heart had known all along.

Lol leaned down and pressed his lips to Rose's, and Rose floated heavenward like a dove. Tingles raced up and down her body. She breathed in deeply, shut her eyes, and lingered within the moment—a too-brief but also just-right experience.

When they parted, Rose's smile faltered. "But poor Coal. You need to save her from her mother."

Crunch. Someone behind them had taken a bite from a piece of fruit. The two lovers turned to find Coal standing against a tree in the shadows. "I am not the one who needs saving, Rose."

"Coal, how long have you been standing there?"

"Too long. Next time, fall in love a bit more quickly."

Coal winked and bit into the apple a second time.

◆ ◆ ◆

Later that day after sundown, Rose entered her cottage and observed Coal seated in a corner reading a scroll of the legends of Kingdom. The candlelight framed the beautiful girl's delicate smile and joyous eyes exactly right. "Did the gardener work late tonight?" Coal asked.

Puzzled, Rose replied with a question of her own. "What do you mean?"

Coal stood and giggled. "For he just delivered the happiest rose on the vine to this cottage."

Rose shook her head. "You are but a poor jester, my friend. Recall that you told Lol and me to spend the day together."

"And I am overjoyed you listened." Cole lifted the candle to illuminate their faces. "You have a sparkle in your eyes I have never seen before."

Rose said, "If I do, it is because I have a solution to your problem. Lol and I agree. We will marry quickly, and you can come live with us."

Coal snorted. "Exactly what a new marriage needs. A

third."

Rose crossed her arms. "You are our best friend. You will be no trouble at all."

"I have a counterproposal," said Coal. "You and Lol court each other for as long as you want, join in marriage when you are ready, and live together without me."

"And how will that help you exactly?" asked Rose.

Coal set the candle on a nearby ledge. "While you have been out, I have thought quite a bit about my situation. 'Tis time I stand up for myself. I will not let my mother control me."

Rose grabbed onto her friend's hands. "That you cannot do. Your mother is a sturdy farmer's wife. Coal dear, she is stronger than you."

"I am not stronger, true." Coal squeezed Rose's hands. "But I have friends—the men and women who work the farm. When I sense my mother is irritable, I will hurry to them and help them with their chores. My mother would never punish me in front of them and risk her reputation. You know that Gillfoyle and Ryssa will not put up with it, and I think my mother is afraid of the new man, Lyken."

Rose's eye twitched. "They will not always be available."

Coal removed her hands and held them high. "Then I shall be a ghost, a person she will overlook. And if I must, I will leave. Do not worry, Rose. 'Tis long overdue I dealt with my mother. All I need is your support."

Rose embraced Coal. "And you have it. Now and forever."

Coal set her head on Rose's shoulder and replied, "Forever and now."

OH WELL

Sprawled on the ground, Radiance Hartstone regarded her wrist and held her breath while waiting for the pain to abate. Her wrist throbbed and turned a tangerine shade of orange while she fought the rising panic, wondering how she could take back the last minute. As a slave, she relied on her hands to work; otherwise, she risked the possibility of a stringent beating.

Daydreaming about words and their definitions, Radiance had lost her balance while climbing the grassy hillside. Her foot had sunk into a shallow gopher hole and her bucket went flying. When the lexicologist-wannabe had flung out her hands to break the fall, she had miscalculated the angle of her descent. Her right hand had twisted with a popping sound upon striking the ground, and a stabbing fire had flared through her nerves.

Radiance tentatively bent her hand and it responded appropriately despite the hot needle-pricks poking her joints. Sighing with relief, she knew the wrist would mend without a healer's magic. As if her family would send for a healer for her.

Radiance rose to her feet, fetched her pail with her good hand, and let her sore wrist hang limply, enduring the pain. While she thought about visiting a healer on her own, the injured girl reflected on her position in the Hartstone family. Even when she was a small child, they had made clear she had been adopted, but they still treated her as a daughter. Of the four family members, Mr. Hartstone had been the kindest to her. Perhaps his compassion stemmed from her being the youngest of the family. Her adoptive father had brought her berries from his walks and gave no special preference to his other daughters over her. Strangely enough, Mrs. Hartstone was the one who had adopted her and brought her home, but the woman had never warmed to Radiance.

Cursing her clumsiness, the girl carried the pail up the hill to the well. Before she fell, she had been worrying about her education and regretting her limited vocabulary. More than anything, she wanted to learn new words and present herself with dignity. All that the family allowed her to say now was "Yes, ma'am" or "I shall not tarry, ma'am."

At times, Radiance had longer and more meaningful conversations with her sister closest in age, Clydamonte. Yet Clyde, initially a friend and confidante, now mocked her in the same way that her eldest sister and her mother did. Clydamonte had changed for the worse ever since their father had died.

The injured girl stumbled to the well with her head down and wrist throbbing. The well's exterior came to the same height as her ribs and comprised a mishmash of pockmarked stones with holes between them large enough to stick your index finger through. The watering hole's construction had no roof, welcoming any rainwater it collected. It came equipped with its own birch bucket tied to a hemp line that had one end connected to a spike in the ground.

Radiance set down her pail and lowered the well's bucket with her uninjured hand, sliding the rope between her fingers. The container descended into the shadows of the hole's gullet, the shaft swallowing it as a monster might a tidbit of a helpless child.

The adopted daughter waited a minute for the water to seep into the bucket and then started to pull it up. As she did, her wrist cried foul, and she dropped the rope and moaned. The slave girl massaged her injured wrist, choking back the tears. *This is bad*, she thought, wishing she knew a word worse than "bad."

"May I help you, miss?"

Turning around in fright, Radiance just barely avoided colliding with a boy behind her. She hadn't heard the stranger approach and now took one step away from him. He, a teenage male, stood immobile, observing her with eyes the color of a watermelon rind. He appeared to be in his mid-teens, perhaps four years past Radiance's age of twelve. He had tousled, brown hair, clean enough to reflect the sunlight. A square chin with a cleft, sideburns, a sun-baked complexion, and an earthy scent screamed "farm boy." He didn't smile but his crinkled eyes and the lines on his forehead demonstrated his concern.

The girl shrank from him, ashamed of her weakness and conscious of her appearance, which featured dirt embedded in her skin and impossible tangles in her hair. She hoped he wouldn't notice the sweat and tearstains running down her face. Her clothes had fit her last year but pressed against her body now. She wore wooden shoes her sister had given her from one of the girl's dolls, and her right wrist bulged like a balloon compared to her left.

"I can manage," she squeaked. "I am no helpless damsel."

She meant it. Radiance was the strongest member of her family. Mrs. Hartstone and her two daughters had grown soft and plump after they'd decided to leave the chores to their adopted servant. Radiance's work, day after day, had left her with a lithe figure and solid muscles.

The slave now turned her back on the boy and tried again. She pulled on the rope, but her wrist first protested then squealed. She managed to lift the birch container a little way but then a searing ache in her joint overwhelmed her, and she dropped the rope once more.

The young man viewed the girl's second failed attempt. "Please, let me help."

Radiance grimaced. "I have hurt my wrist. I have drawn water from this well many times. This time, because of an accident, I am unable to do so."

"Yes, I have seen you here before," the boy said. "You do not have to prove your strength to me. I wish to accomplish your task and then begin mine."

She recognized him then. He belonged to the Jolly estate, a large, bustling farm to the east. The Hartstones lived comfortably from the produce of a small estate, but the Jollys possessed multiple farms and were well-to-do.

Resigning herself to accepting his help, Radiance stepped back. "Very well."

The boy grabbed the rope and yanked on it, easily lifting the vessel of water. As he pulled, Radiance considered the Jolly estate and what working there would be like. "You are a slave on the Jolly farm. Do they treat you properly?"

He eyed her, and she blushed at her pronunciation of the word starting with an "s." He stopped tugging on the rope for a moment. "Did you say the word 'slave'?" he asked.

She gritted her teeth. "I have something called a lisp. My father took me to a healer when I was a child. I cannot do anything about it."

He returned to his work. "I do not care how people talk."

"And I do not care how you judge me, farmhand."

The boy raised the pail and set it on the ledge. She reached for the bucket to pour its contents into her own pail, but he warded her off. "I will do it."

"No. 'Tis a simple chore."

He grabbed the sides of the birch bucket and lifted it. "I do not believe you are helpless, only in need of assistance. If I needed help, I would gladly accept it."

She stepped aside, and the youngster carefully poured the water from the well into her container. She grabbed the pail's handle with her left hand, her less dominant side, and lifted it.

"Despite the insult, you have been kind. I wish I could tell the Jollys how nice you have been to me so you might avoid any punishment for being late."

The lad's composed expression turned cheerful, making him appear dashing and exposing a dimple Radiance hadn't noticed before. He lifted the well's instrument to draw his own supply of water. "Let me fetch my water and then I shall carry your bucket back for you."

"In truth, I can do it."

"I have no doubt. However, you may strain your wrist further. Look at it."

The bruise had become an ugly blue, the same shade as thunderstorm clouds. Without further remark, the boy turned to the well and went to work. "Where do you live?"

"The Hartstone farm."

His face hardened while he waited for the water to collect in the bucket below. "I know them, but I have never seen you there."

She wanted to say she was their daughter. A few years prior, she might have claimed kinship with the family, but she didn't dare to do so now. "I am a scullery maid." Her mother referred to Radiance in such a manner, though her chores extended far beyond the kitchen.

"This explains why I have not seen you at the Jolly festival. Mrs. Astoria Hartstone is the lady, I recall. She has two daughters."

Radiance refused to say their formal names, preferring their more common ones. "Nita and Clyde."

"Ah, yes." He poured the contents of the birch bucket into his own and then lifted both containers. "Lead the way, m'lady."

Radiance released a deep breath, and she blushed with frustration as she proceeded down the hill. "Bad luck is my best friend. I fell on my wrist. Otherwise—"

"Otherwise, you could do this yourself. I am well aware."

"I wish I had not stumbled."

The young man stepped alongside her and matched her pace. "You should have said so back at the well."

"What do you mean?"

The farmhand tossed his head and gestured back to the top of the hill. "Has nobody told you the place we drew water is a wishing well?"

Her eyes narrowed. "It is not true."

"I did not say I believed it, but many around here do. If you speak your innermost wish down the well, it will come to pass."

"How is that possible?"

"Have you never encountered magic before?" the young man asked.

Radiance avoided the gopher hole on her way down. "I have heard of spell wielders but have never met one."

"If you traveled to the left of the sun when it rises, you would encounter Faerie Forest where all sorts of magic exists."

"I have not traveled far beyond our farm. Be so kind as to tell me about the well."

As they marched across the heath and crunched dead gorse branches under their shoes, he related the tale. "There once was a giantess named Soro. Soro was uncommon among giants because she was tall—even for their race. She towered above the other giants. She was fair, not born with a pug nose or thick eyebrows as was the lot of many of her kin."

"She had only one head?"

"Yes, and it was pleasing to the eye. However, because of her natural beauty and her singular head, she was an outcast. Though height brings privilege, she found herself wandering among human farms. She ended her journey in a cave near Farmer Shagtooth's land and kept to herself, until one day when she saw, and fell in love, with a man named Gerome."

Radiance snorted. "I see where this is going."

"In those days, the neighborhood well was further away and Gerome spent most of his days lugging water back and forth. He wanted a well on his own property. Soro overheard this, and she began digging a well for him, hoping her action would please him, and he would fall in love with her. She dug every night while he slept and hid during the day. Gerome thought fairies were helping him, never dreaming it was a Titaness."

Radiance held up a hand to interrupt him. "I am unfamiliar with that term. Does it mean giantess?"

"Indeed, it does."

Pleased with herself that she had learned a new word, Radiance tucked the term into her memory, repeating it three times.

Balancing the buckets in either hand, the storyteller continued. "Soro presented herself to Gerome upon completing the well. Displeased the reclusive female giant had been his benefactress, Gerome demanded she withdraw from his property. Instead, she leaned over the well and cried, heartbroken, and filled the depths with her tears. Though he had rejected her, she told him the well was like her love. It would never run dry. People believe her spirit grants wishes to the heartbroken."

Radiance rolled her eyes. "What a load of rubbish."

"I am but repeating the legend."

The Hartstones' youngest shaded her eyes and held out her arm for her companion to stop. "We are within sight of my mistress's house, and Clyde is about. I will carry the pail from here. I promise to rest my wrist as I can."

The boy presented her with her bucket while eyeing the farm in the distance. "You are afraid Mrs. Hartstone will see me?"

"And punish me for laziness."

The boy inclined his head. "I would tell you to give her my best, but I would be lying."

Radiance said, "If I knew how to write, I would send the Jolly family a note telling how kind you have been. If I happen to meet them at my mistress's house, I will mention you. My name is Radiance. What is your name?"

"Roger."

"Well, Mr. Roger, I thank you for your aid. 'Tis appreciated."

Radiance scurried away from the boy as quickly as possible. Not speaking often to strangers...or anyone for that matter...she had welcomed the company. Now the slave strolled across the heath toward her sister, not glancing back but reflecting on the encounter. The farmhand had good manners for a servant boy.

Her sister Clyde approached Radiance, eyes blazing. "What were you doing with *him*?"

"His name is Roger. He helped me after I hurt my wrist."

She expected Clyde to call her clumsy or helpless, but instead, her sister put her hands on her hips. "I recognized him from a distance. He is one of the Jolly boys. The younger one, Roger Jolly."

Radiance worked as hard as her wrist allowed for the rest of the day. Clyde, her confidante years before, decided to question her at different intervals. She wanted to know what Roger Jolly was like and why he had carried her water home. The Hartstones' "scullery maid" told the story again and again, with Clyde listening, but not helping her with her chores.

Clyde stopped to take a breath after complimenting Roger with no fewer than ten adjectives. Radiance rolled her head dismissively. "He is a simple farmer."

"Shows how little you know. The Jollys are one of the richest families around and are on the brink of prominence. If a family has wealth for three generations, they may ascend to nobility. Roger's grandfather bought out all his neighbors and turned into the wealthiest man in the county."

Thrilled by the revelation that she had talked to a boy so near nobility, Radiance hummed to herself for the rest of the afternoon. Roger had treated her with respect—a rare occurrence in her world these days. If they met again, she would reciprocate his benevolence.

Roger was waiting near the well the next day when she arrived. Dressed in a ragged tunic with a hand scratching his windblown hair, he leaned casually against the stone well. She again perceived him as an ordinary farmhand; however, the sun behind him created a halo around his body. The way he held his head high and threw his shoulders back demonstrated his good breeding.

Radiance curtsied as she approached him, cheeks flushing with color when she remembered how she had treated him the day before. He pulled up his bucket while Radiance waited behind him, once glancing over his shoulder and grinning. She decided to speak to break the awkwardness. "I apologize for my rude behavior yesterday, Mr. Jolly. I thought you were on my level."

He retrieved the bucket from the well and poured the water into his receptacle. "Your level?"

"Your family approaches nobility, and I am but a slave."

"And yet we are equals in the eyes of God. How fares your wrist?"

Radiance hid her injury behind her back. "Fine."

He peered at her, and she realized he wouldn't continue on until he examined her wrist. Removing her hand from behind her back, she presented it to him. He held it with a light touch as if cradling a baby bird. "It does not look fine to me. Did you rest it?"

"I had chores to do."

"I will draw your water and carry your pail for you again today." She was about to protest, but he tilted his chin to the side. "Do not argue with near-nobility."

She crossed her arms while Roger set about to draw Radiance's portion of the well's riches. The bucket splashed into the water as he turned to her. "Besides, after consolation, friends should help one another when they are hurt."

Radiance blinked. "Friends?"

"I enjoyed talking to you yesterday. As the owner's son, everyone on the farm is guarded around me. I cannot bear it. I want people to speak plainly to me."

"You were more friendly to me than I was to you, Mr. Jolly."

"Please call me Roger, and you are welcome to be a bit friendlier at any time."

He poured the contents of the well's bucket into Radiance's

container, and they started their journey toward the Hartstones' farm. The girl made her way down the hill while watching her feet, not wanting to trip in front of her new friend. "My sister Clyde saw you yesterday and wanted to know about you."

"Tell her we are friends, and if she is ever demeaning toward you, I will refuse to dance with her. She asks me at every festival."

"I dare not cross her."

"Are they mean to you, Little One?"

Radiance felt vexed at the pet name. "I will not speak against the Hartstones."

"They are jealous. You have golden hair to their dark features and blue eyes to their gray. And a name like Radiance is far better than Nita and Clyde."

Radiance kicked a bramble out of the way as they traveled across the heath. "Oh, they do not call me by my real name."

"What do they call you?"

"All manner of names. I do not wish to discuss them."

"As you say," he replied.

"Do you think you will become a noble?"

"Possibly. The family has had money for three generations. My brother and I might advance."

"You have a brother?"

"My elder. He will inherit most of the farm, but my father plans to leave me a generous share as well. My brother is my best friend, anyway. He wants to split the farm in half. An equal share for each of us."

Glassy-eyed, Radiance stared at the clouds. "Having a brother you trust must be wonderful."

"'Tis. Who awaits us ahead?"

Radiance gasped as she observed Clyde, her older sister, and her mother standing at the edge of their property. She grabbed the bucket and started away. "I must be going. I enjoyed walking with you."

As she ran toward her farm, he called out softly, "I did not get you in trouble, did I?"

She shook her head and rushed forward, knowing her fate before she arrived. They would question her, become enraged with her answers no matter what she said, and double her chores. She hurried toward their grim faces filled with judgment and scorn.

◆ ◆ ◆

After she wiped the kitchen floor clean, Radiance sat up and set her brush aside. The immaculate floor met with her approval when she ran a finger along the stones. Then the clip-clop of Mrs. Hartstone's shoes caught her attention, and her mistress walked across her work, leaving muddy tracks behind. Radiance bit her lip to suppress her frustration.

Mrs. Hartstone leaned down and blocked her stepdaughter's view with her round, olive-green eyes and pinched mouth. She examined the floor washer as she might a bug she'd captured in a jar. "I did not see you there, Miss Filth."

"I will clean it again."

"Naturally, but not right now. I wish to speak to you." The elder Hartstone straightened up, apparently expecting her stepdaughter to do the same. Radiance put her brush in her bucket but didn't rise.

"Stand and face me."

After Radiance rose to her feet, Mrs. Hartstone took her adopted daughter's chin in her hand and squeezed it. "You are an impertinent thing, talking to that boy. I do not want you to speak to him again."

"I did not seek him out. We met by chance at the well."

"Perhaps I should send Clyde to the well tomorrow."

Radiance stifled a derisive snort, picturing Clyde drawing water and struggling to carry the heavy pail. Oh, what was she thinking? Clyde would make Radiance lug the bucket back and forth. Why did the Hartstones have to ruin her trips to the well? She wanted to talk to Roger, her only friend in the world, alone.

When Radiance didn't answer, Mrs. Hartstone released her.

"I warn you not to talk to him again."

"I am not speaking ill of you or anyone else." The instant the words left her mouth, Radiance, regretting voicing her thoughts, winced.

"Of course you are. Do you think I am gullible? What could he possibly want to talk to you about except our affairs? He is using you to get to know about the rest of us, Pigsnouta."

The daughter refrained from denying her mother's theory and dropped her eyes instead, grateful her mistress wasn't a mind reader.

"Attend to me." Mrs. Hartstone grabbed the girl's chin again and tugged it forward. "If you see him at the well tomorrow, avoid it. Go to the well at Landsbark."

The Landsbark well was two miles further and Radiance internally groaned at the thought of carrying water all the way home from there. Mrs. Hartstone would scold her for her tardiness, and she would have to work harder to cook the meal with her injured wrist. Traveling to that distant well was not fair! Yet she knew better than to talk back.

Mrs. Hartstone turned and walked away, her filthy shoes further muddying the floor.

When Radiance approached the well the next day, she didn't see anyone nearby. A flock of swallows flew overhead, and their diminutive shadows raced across her body. She climbed the hill leading to the well, rubbing her sore wrist. As she reached for the rope, she hesitated and regretted she had missed him this time.

Roger's head poked up from the other side of the well's wall. He had been out of her line of sight until then. He said, "Hello again."

Radiance's eyes widened. "My mistress has forbidden me to talk to you."

'Fine. I shall talk to you instead. You do not need to speak."

"She will make me go to a different well if we continue to meet here."

"Draw your water and sit with me on this side of the well. I have been resting in the shade. 'Tis a pleasant day." He sat back down on the far side of the circular wall.

"I must get back to the Hartstones."

"Will they miss you? Do they not think you are traveling to a distant location?"

Radiance set her canister on the ground and lowered the well pail into the darkness below. From behind the well, Roger's voice floated through the air. "It is nice and cool down here."

Radiance's bucket settled in the liquid and filled with water. "Why do you wish to talk to me?"

"This is what friends do, Little One. They talk to each other."

"I hate the name 'Little One.' How dare you call me little? I am a couple of inches smaller than you and not much younger. The name is as awful as the names they call me back at home."

Roger's eyes appeared over the lip of the well's wall. "You misunderstand me. I refer to our faith. The Little Ones are people with a pure faith, the humble and obedient. Their prayers are heard and granted and do more than all the soldiers in the king's army. It is an apt description of you, Miss Radiance."

Radiance blinked. "I am no saint."

"Not much of a sinner, either."

She poured the water into her pail, and then her eyes met his. "I suppose I have a couple of minutes."

She set down the pail and sat next to Roger in the shadow of the well. The umbra kept the heat of the sun off them, and the temperature was the lazy warmth of a pleasant summer day. Roger leaned his head against the wall and closed his eyes. "Is this not more agreeable?"

Radiance tilted her face from the shadows allowing the sunlight to fall on her cheeks. "'Tis. However, a noble should not meet with a slave."

"I care not a whit for nobility. I do not care for the festivals they throw, the pompous ways they treat each other, or the titles they hold."

"'Tis irresponsible. You are declining a great privilege."

Roger's eyes glazed over. "True. One aspect of having a title appeals to me. I could influence Kingdom and make it glorious once more. My father talks often about how Kingdom used to be. The times when giant and man, dwarf and gnome, elf and goblin lived in peace. Trolls didn't threaten travelers, sailors didn't sell mermaids into slavery, and soldiers rode dragons into battle. I want to restore our world to one of harmony."

"And you will accomplish this?"

Roger picked up a leaf and flipped it back and forward between his thumb and forefinger. "God's heaven, not alone. King Shade leads his soldiers admirably, and he needs boys like me to accomplish grand tasks. And he needs girls like you who are true of heart."

"To cook and clean?"

"What do you think of me, Little One? My mother fought ogres in the Marsh of Wishes. No, they need people like us defending what is right. King Shade promises to restore Kingdom once more, and I believe him."

Roger's optimism captivated her. Back at the Hartstones' homestead, her mother and her sisters complained day and night about their misfortune. Now his words set fire to her imagination of a better future—but not for long. She recalled her station. "The world may change, but my days will always be the same."

Roger shook his head. "If we restore harmony to Kingdom, I suspect the king will abolish slavery. You will be free."

"The Hartstones will never set me free."

"In a land of plenty, what need will we have for slavery?"

"I appreciate your consolation," said Radiance, recalling the new word she'd learned from him the previous day. "The Hartstones do not want for money. Mrs. Hartstone keeps me under her watchful eye for another reason. May I confess something to you?"

"Please."

"I feel as though she keeps me prisoner there."

She expected him to ridicule her, but he didn't. His eyes became focused on a spot on the ground. "I dislike your mistress. When we bought her second farm after her husband died, I did not like how she dealt with my father. She is a greedy, selfish woman, and I would not be surprised if she has some ulterior motive for keeping you."

Thrilled to have someone agree with her, Radiance continued. "The reason for my..."

"Captivity?" he offered.

She glowed with hearing a new word. "Yes. I thought it was my imagination, but saying it aloud and your belief in what I believe...I cannot tell you what it means to me!"

Gratitude for his compassion overwhelmed her, and Radiance found herself longing to stay with him. Her heart quavered like a plucked harp string. The conversation might have gone in a dozen different directions, but Roger's affirmation of her suspicions made all the difference in the world to her. He validated her deepest emotions, cementing her affection for him.

The two companions talked about the future of Kingdom for an hour until Radiance realized how much time had passed. She hurried away, thanking him for the respite. Beaded eyes and pursed lips greeted her when she arrived home. When Mrs. Hartstone asked her why she was late, she said she'd had to use the Landsbark well because of "that boy."

Radiance had never fibbed to Mrs. Hartstone and was surprised her mother believed her this time. The girl carried on with her chores for the rest of the day, ignoring the pain in her wrist and humming the songs the doves chirped to her in the morning.

◆ ◆ ◆

As she grabbed her pail to collect water the next day, Radiance jumped, frightened by Mrs. Hartstone's sudden appearance, which destroyed her sunny mood. Her mother, her ice-colored hair matching her frozen glare, stepped in front of the door. "I think Clydamonte should accompany you to the well today."

"She does not need to, ma'am."

Radiance went to sidestep her, but Mrs. Hartstone blocked her passage again. "Yet Clydamonte will go with you anyway, and all that matters is what I think."

As usual, Radiance had to concede to her mistress's whims, and Radiance and Clyde set off together on their peregrination. Her sister's sidelong glances brought down Radiance's earlier upbeat mood like the sudden appearance of mischievous brownies on a picnic day. Radiance supposed the situation could have been worse, though—Mrs. Hartstone might have chosen Nita as her companion.

They marched across the heath, not remarking on the faint smell of lavender or the humid kiss of moisture on their cheeks. When they approached the well, Radiance spotted Roger pouring water into his own bucket. This prompted a sudden thought. "There he is! We should go to Landsbark and avoid that pompous farm boy."

Clyde's eyes widened. "He is handsome, is he not? Let us draw water from this well. I shall not tell mother."

The youngest Hartstone would rather have gone out of her way than greet Roger with her sister, but she complied with her sister's wishes the same way she had her entire life. She trudged up the hill, with Clyde bouncing on the balls of her feet beside her.

Spying their approach, Roger waited for them and focused on Clyde. "Hello, Little One. Who have you brought today?"

Radiance approached the well and grabbed the hemp rope to start her chore. "This is Clydamonte as if you did not know. She is here to make sure a rogue does not accost me."

Roger bowed and took Clyde's hand. "What a lovely warden. It is nice to meet you on this beautiful day."

Clyde blushed. "'Tis my pleasure."

Radiance flushed with his attention to her sister and lowered her bucket, taking a deep breath to calm herself. Roger addressed Clyde while Radiance worked. "We have danced at festivals. How fares your other sister?"

Clyde's smile faltered. "She is back home. You are a wonderful dancer."

Radiance groaned mentally at the trite compliment.

"I care little for festivals," Roger confessed. "However if maidens as pretty as the two of you frequent them, maybe I should attend more often."

The middle Hartstone daughter tittered at the response while Radiance seethed. Roger's praise was meant for her, not Clyde. Her odious sister was stealing her time with him. She wanted to crown the other girl's head with her bucket.

Clyde and Roger continued their discussion while Radiance set about completing her task. They engaged in idle chit-chat, and Roger continued to pay the lion's share of attention to her sister. When Radiance started to tip the water into her bucket, he offered to do the chore for her.

"I am more than capable of pouring water," she snapped.

Roger stepped back. "You are in a foul mood today."

That statement didn't improve her temperament at all. Now she wanted to swing the pail at *his* head.

Their chores completed, Roger offered his arm to Radiance on one side and Clyde on the other. "Let me escort the two of you back to your farm."

The youngest Hartstone drew away a step. What if Mrs. Hartstone saw her having her arm entwined with that of the Jolly estate heir? Not hesitating, however, Clyde looped her arm with Roger's, and so Radiance coiled her arm in his as well, not about to be left behind. Roger accompanied them down the hill.

As they crossed the heath, Roger cleared his throat. "Well, Little One, and Little One's sister, I have a surprise for the two of you."

Radiance, who had never cared for the moniker, found herself angry that she shared it with her sister now. That was *her* annoying pet name!

Clyde's voice squeaked as irritating as a rusty door hinge. "And that is?"

"I have decided to join the king's soldiers. After our talk

yesterday, Radiance, you inspired me to do my part. I did not wait for the king's request. I welcome the day I will lead men into battle."

Radiance glared at him as they stepped off of the hill and onto the heath. "You jest."

"No. Kingdom needs men like me. We must fight with haste, else lose all."

Radiance gripped his arm. "I hope you are not eager for battle."

"Only with those whose cause is not just. Radiance, you are troubled?"

"Troubled? Why would I be? If you want to rush into war and lose your life, it is your choice, not mine."

Roger turned his full attention to her. "Do you really feel that way?"

She tried to impart her thoughts into his mind. Of course not! He must know by now how much she looked forward to meeting him at the well and that she secretly prayed at night for him to be there the next day. Or how her pulse quickened whenever she saw him.

Clyde batted her eyelashes at him. "I think it is honorable for a man to fight for his king. You are certain to be the best."

Roger squared his shoulders. "How nice of you to say so."

The slave girl swallowed a lump of regret that she hadn't taken the opportunity to compliment him. If she had supported his decision, though, she would've been lying. She didn't want him to go away. She wanted to meet him every day at Soro's. She wanted for him to remain here, safe from battles and wars. Her body tensed to think of him in danger, picturing trolls with blood-filled eyes surrounding him.

"You should not go." Radiance accidentally spoke the thought aloud.

Roger released her arm. "Why?"

She wanted to tell him he was not yet a man, that he needed to experience more of life before he went off to war. He shouldn't be a pawn in a king's hand. "You may be killed."

"Oh, Raddy," said Clyde who had never before called Radiance this ridiculous name in her life. "You are so silly. Roger shall be the best of all soldiers. How can he lead an army one day if he never fights in one?"

"I like how you think, Miss Clydamonte."

"Please, call me Clyde." The Hartstone daughter giggled.

Radiance wanted to call her sister something all right, but such a word shouldn't be uttered in polite company. Her frustration boiled over the side of her pot of tolerance. If her simpering sister hadn't been there, she could have spoken her mind.

The three of them continued their journey, and Radiance retained her control, knowing it the best course of action. She watched her world crumble away as Roger spent the rest of the time speaking about small matters with Clyde. All the way home, Radiance sensed a chasm growing between herself and the king's volunteer. She had lost her influence on Roger for the Jolly heir had dismissed Radiance from his life.

As the Hartstone residence came into view, Roger wished a pleasant day to both of them. He turned and walked toward his own home, and Clyde danced off in the opposite direction. Radiance didn't follow her sister, though; instead, she stood in the field and watched her confidante march to his doom.

The next day, a determined Radiance snuck away without Clyde. She decided to go to the well a little earlier than usual and wait for Roger. If her sister made her way to the well at all, she would be late.

Radiance thus journeyed forth with her pail, hoping to have a few words alone with Roger to dissuade him from enlisting. While the girl understood her friend's need for glory, she brooded that he hadn't thought of all possible outcomes of becoming a soldier. Kingdom could be an unforgiving world.

Radiance arrived at the well as the noon sun's golden eye focused its attention on the landscape. She steadied herself against the wall and drew water. Hiding on the other side of the well where Roger had once sat, she waited as the sun moved across the sky to the time when the youth usually arrived. After a while, she stood, poured the water back into the well, hummed to herself, and drew the water again to occupy her time. Repeating this action three more times, the water-gatherer grew more and more concerned. She waited twice as long as it would take her to draw water, knowing she would be blamed for laziness. No Roger.

Resigned, the distraught girl lugged her bucket of water down the hill and across the heath, scattering butterflies as she made her way home. She was worried—he wasn't the type to miss an encounter. She chewed her lip as she strolled across the grasslands of the Hartstone farm, then went in through the back door and resumed her duties.

Nita crossed the slave's path as she scrubbed the kitchen walls. "Where have you been, Your Lispness?"

Radiance ignored the insult. "Fetching water."

"All this time? Did you crawl to the well?"

Radiance didn't say a word. Nita didn't speak to her unless necessary, so she must have wanted to talk to Radiance for some reason. Her eldest sister leaned against the wall but kept her attention on the other room as if embarrassed to confide in the servant. "You missed all of the excitement, Dogface. Roger Jolly called on Clyde this morning, and they are out walking."

Radiance stopped cleaning in mid-motion. Regarding the back of her sister's head, she uttered one word. "Truly?"

"Is it not awful? Why her? I am the eldest, more beautiful, more eligible. I do not know why he favors her."

A lump formed in Radiance's throat. He had skipped the meeting with her to be with her cruel mistress's daughter. Her heart sank as she reflected on the news, knowing Nita wouldn't make up a story where she wasn't the center of attention.

Nita bit the inside of her cheek then noticed Radiance. "You look upset, Troll Lips. Why?"

"I am not upset."

Her sister's eyes flashed. "You favored him, did you not?

Our dear little Lady Stench had hopes that a landowner might marry a slave." She cackled, a cross between a cat's wail and a dog's whimper. "Wait until I tell Mother."

Radiance wanted to beg her to keep quiet, but she knew asking anything of her sister was pointless. Nita rushed from the kitchen, and the slave girl's shoulders sagged. She dropped to her knees, dipped her towel into her bucket, and scrubbed the floors, mixing the bucket water with her tears.

While Radiance was preparing the evening meal, her family gathered in the front room. Roger could be heard among them. Upset and disappointed, Radiance gripped the wooden spoon, refusing to eavesdrop. She stirred the stew as she added carrots. A shriek of joy jarred her, and then Clyde shouted. "Raddy! Come here, Raddy!"

Radiance closed her eyes. Again with the "Raddy" nickname, and it sounded more like "Ratty" than "Raddy." She wanted to ignore her sister but knew if she didn't attend to her, Clyde would tell their mother. And if Mrs. Hartstone discovered Radiance had disobeyed a direct order, her mother would punish her severely.

The "scullery maid" put down her utensils and walked as calmly as she could into the front room. Clyde sat on a high-backed chair, and Roger stood beside her. Radiance entered and curtsied, keeping her eyes focused on the ground. "I am stirring the stew and it will boil away if I do not attend to it."

Clyde giggled. "Let the stew set for a moment, Raddy. Our neighbor Roger wishes to speak to you."

Radiance turned toward Roger, not daring to raise her eyes. Roger bowed his head to move into her line of sight. "How are you, Radiance?"

"Fine, thank you."

"Your eyes are all bloodshot! Have you been crying?"

"The wildflowers bother me. I walked through them on my way home from the well...alone."

Roger scuffed his shoe against the floor. "I am sorry I did not see you there today."

He opened his mouth to say something else, but Clyde loudly interrupted him. "He was spending the majority of the day with *me!*"

Radiance twisted her ragged apron in her hands. "May I return to the stew?"

Roger inclined his head. "It was nice to see you just now, Radiance."

Curtsying, she left but she didn't make it back to the kitchen before her eyes welled up. She hated how Clyde had said "me." She hated Nita for guessing her feelings for Roger. She hated everyone, and returned to the stew, dabbing at her eyes to keep her tears from mixing with the food.

The next day, Radiance made her way across the heath and trudged to the wall of the well, dispirited. She set her bucket on the ledge but startled and nearly dropped it when Roger peeked around the corner. "Greetings, Little One."

Sniffing, Radiance lowered the bucket into the water. Roger stood and moved around to her side of the well. "Do you want me to raise the pail for you?"

"I can draw water myself, thank you. I have been doing it without you for many years."

Roger stepped back and allowed Radiance to continue. She poured the water without acknowledging his presence. He set his hand next to hers on the stone lip. "Why are you upset with me?"

Radiance shook with frustration. What a thing to ask her. She wanted to say, "I am not upset with you at all." Or, "I am not myself today." She opened her mouth, trying to decide which guarded statement to use, but what emerged was as much a surprise to her as it was to him.

"How could you? How could you come to my house and enjoy the company of the people who treat me horribly? They call me names and make me wait on them hand and foot. I thought you were my friend!"

She yelled the last sentence, a little spittle striking his chin. He retrieved a handkerchief and wiped it away, his eyes never leaving hers. "I am your friend, Radiance."

She shook at his calm tone and use of her name. "Clyde is horrible to me."

"Was she ill-tempered with you last night?"

Radiance shook her head.

"Were any of them?"

Again, she shook her head.

"I wonder why?"

Radiance's eyes widened. "You told her to be nice to me?"

"And to influence her family as well. The way they treat you...it is not right. I also made sure she will no longer accompany you to the well."

"Oh, do you know what you have done? Do you know what Clyde thinks?"

Roger grabbed the crook of his right arm with his left hand. "She is a lonely girl in need of a friend. I befriended her. What more is there to it?"

Radiance had never thought of her mistress's daughter as lonely. The revelation gave her new insight into the depths of Roger's concern for others, and her anger dissipated. At the same time, she thought him the most naïve boy she had ever met.

"She is attracted to you, and you act as if it is possible to pair with her."

Roger's jaw clenched. "You jest."

Radiance put her hand on her chest. "Upon my honor."

Roger brushed his hair back. "But this is terrible. I never meant for her to think I was courting her. I was only being friendly. Why would she think of me as a sweetmate?"

Exasperated, Radiance threw her hands into the air. "Why would she be interested? You are handsome, wealthy, kind to a fault, and courageous, signing up to be a soldier."

"I never intended to woo any girl." The farm heir scuffed his boot heel in the dirt. "I am but fifteen years of age."

"Old enough to marry, Roger. Clyde approaches the marrying age of fourteen. Such a joining is not out of the question."

"I am not interested in romancing any maiden. I was being myself."

Of course, he was. Caring, honorable...handsome. She would hate him if he acted any other way, but his confession spoke to her as well. He viewed her as a friend and nothing more.

"I must distance myself from her," said Roger. "But I must continue to meet with her for your sake. She needs a friend. I believe she is a kind person. Do you agree?"

When they were younger, Clyde and Radiance had been best friends, but after her father's death, her mother and Nita had changed Clyde's heart. Yet Radiance recalled an event a couple of weeks ago when Clyde made excuses to her mother for a meal Radiance had burned. Other similar incidents came to mind. "I do."

"Good. I have a month before I report. I will tell her to be nice to you, and I will meet you as often as I am able."

"A month!" Radiance closed her eyes, knowing what she was about to say might threaten their relationship. "I want you to remain a farmer and not become a soldier."

Roger reared back. "But why?"

"Because, as my...friend, I do not wish harm to come to you. In the heat of battle with the enemies of Kingdom, you may be killed. It pains me to think of it!"

Roger reached out and took her hands. His soft touch set a tingle along Radiance's arm. "Little One, you know how Kingdom works. If you are honorable, if your cause is true, if you fight on the right side, you shall be victorious. What could go wrong?"

"Even innocents are killed."

"You worry too much. I am a master swordsman. My father made sure of it. I believe in myself and my cause. Will you not believe in me?"

His supplication touched her in such a special way that she didn't know how to respond. Her heart told her one thing—her mind, another. She wanted to believe in him, and in the end, she knew he was resolved to fight for the king. "Yes, I believe."

"I will bring you back tales of triumph. I promise."

He lifted the bucket and talked to her about his future plans as they strolled down the hill.

A month and many conversations later, Radiance again journeyed to the wishing well for her water. Gray clouds spread across the sky, reflecting her current mood. She swung her pail as she made her way across the heath.

Yesterday, she had said farewell to Roger. He had ridden off to training and patrol duty, and then onto whatever role the king desired. He was excited, speaking of subduing dragons and killing trolls, his voice rising louder and louder. She pictured him talking next to the well, waving his arms, and explaining how honored he felt wearing his new uniform. He had claimed he didn't deserve it, and at the same time, quoted many heroes throughout the ages.

Radiance arrived at the base of the hill, regretting she hadn't revealed her feelings for him. She had wanted to throw her arms around him and kiss him good-bye on the cheek, but instead, she had curtsied. He wouldn't have had appreciated the fond gesture. His head remained fixed in the thunderclouds of war, not the gentle, puffy clouds of romance.

She closed her eyes as she lowered the well's bucket and recalled the previous night. She'd had trouble falling asleep on the hard floor, thinking about Roger in battle, and then she had awoken ill at ease to her mother's screeching summons.

Radiance had wept on and off the entire day and now presaged another bout coming on. She sniffed as she poured the well bucket's contents into her own pail and then released the wooden bucket. A lump the size of a goose egg formed in her throat, and she could contain herself no longer and sobbed. She kneeled, put her arms on the side of the well, and buried her face in her hands. Tears rolled down her face. She missed him, worried about him, loved him.

When she hitched her breath enough to speak, Radiance said, "Wishing well, I have a wish. My wish comes from the bottom of my heart, but it does not concern my own personal welfare." Now the words rushed out, intense and raw. "Please...please protect Roger Jolly from meeting his death on the battlefield. Please watch over him and keep him alive."

The world fell silent after her plea, and the girl wiped away the tears that had dripped down her face. Before she turned to leave, a female voice rose from the depths of the well. "He shall live, Little One."

Alarmed, Radiance fell back and nearly rolled down the hill. Her mouth hung down as she stood and stared into the dark emptiness of the well. No one hid at the bottom or anywhere within eyesight, indeed. The servant girl bit her lip and debated what she might say next. Eventually, she decided on the most straightforward answer. "Thank you," she said.

Radiance then collected her pail and held her head high as she walked down toward the heath. She would suffer the insults, the chores, and all the other petty tasks her family asked of her now. All the degradation in the world would be worthwhile in order to be once more, someday, reunited with her friend.

DO NOT SAVE
THE PRINCESS

Lyken talked to the voice in his head, but this didn't make him crazy.

Even in the fairytale domain of Kingdom, speaking to oneself was often associated with insanity, so Lyken kept his conversations under his breath. He had a name for the voice—Bradley—a gentleman much like himself, yet older and wiser. Lyken, when faced with a difficult decision, often consulted him. Today, he murmured to his "advisor" about the spectacle before him.

"Will you look at that, Bradley?"

Lyken observed Lord and Lady Helvys' procession march out of the castle to christen a new ship in the town of Nor. The proud, straight-backed soldiers; the ornate ladies-in-waiting; and the lord who thought himself the king of this province sauntered past. Lord Helvys along the way lifted his hand to the crowd.

Lyken found a leader's waving to his people quite refreshing, so unlike the habit of the king in Lyken's native nation, who didn't acknowledge the commoners at all.

The previous day, Lyken had escaped the land of Kingdom to the smaller territory of Nor, and began noticing the differences immediately. The wooden structures with their earthen tones and round edges were quite foreign to him. He was used to soaring castles and cobblestones in cities, not squat buildings and dirt paths.

But a displaced people would have an unusual architecture, Lyken reasoned. The residents of Nor had appeared out of the mist many years before, settling here. They had wanted to rule Kingdom and had conducted a so-far unsuccessful campaign against their neighbor to expand Nor's boundaries.

The procession now continued down the street, and Lyken whispered, "Why have I come here?"

Bradley didn't answer, but Lyken knew how he would most likely respond. Lyken *had* to be here. He had wronged a powerful woman, a woman of means and connections, although he had done the right thing. Four days earlier, he had run from her hired assassins, hiding near the Circle of Counsel.

Bradley had advised Lyken to disappear, and Lyken had agreed. He'd headed north into the Forest of Death, keeping to hidden trails until he reached the territory of Nor. Lyken knew the assassins wouldn't follow him here, though his decision was not without peril. Lord Helvys liked nothing better than to expose a spy from Kingdom and execute him publicly.

"What am I doing here, Bradley? The lord will never believe I have abandoned Kingdom."

Again, no answer. Bradley wasn't always available, something Lyken found quite irritating.

Behind the lord and lady strode their only daughter. Chin raised and eyes blazing, she wore an egg-yolk-yellow dress with ebony trim. In her black boots, her steps were entirely sure-footed, despite a three-inch heel. A black belt wrapped around her waist, while ruining the elegant appearance of the dress, nonetheless provided a quite practical purpose. The belt held three effective weapons: a short sword, a throwing dagger, and a ball-and-spikes flail. The girl was simply not a typical heir apparent.

Lyken had heard tales concerning the daughter, Helga Helvys—for her very name spread fear far and wide across Kingdom. While most citizens of Kingdom didn't want the lord and lady of Nor to rule them, having Helga as their leader was completely unthinkable. Acknowledged as an accomplished fighter, though she was still even younger than twenty years, she was viewed a tyrant by her own people.

The whispered stories claimed Helga had single-handedly killed three ferocious giants in battle and had mounted their heads on her bedroom walls. She was well known for not showing mercy to her subjects, and, indeed, would play cruel tricks on them. They called her a supernatural creature—only *appearing* to be human—who desired power above all else.

Lyken had never seen the young lady before. She had a ruddy complexion and dark hair with three braids bouncing against her back. The severe expression, combined with a knitted brow and imperious glare at the throng, supported the rumors. She was not someone to be crossed.

Lyken's initial impression was not flattering. *She is the type to pull a man's arms out for sport. If I am caught and stand in the gallows, she is not—*

"Death to evil despots!"

The howl rang out from the roof of a nearby market, and everyone turned toward the speaker, but Lyken knew the cry was a ruse. His hunter's instinct guided him to look in the opposite direction. The man who had shouted the treasonous words was on Lyken's side of the road, and the procession sought him out, but when they turned their heads, a woman emerged from an alleyway and readied an arrow. Lyken had thought that surely others around him saw the archer, but the mob craned their necks upward, hoping to catch a glimpse of the person who had yelled the protest. Only Lyken had remained focused across the street.

The bow-woman, hair parted down the middle with blonde locks on her left and black on her right, aimed her arrow, and Lyken knew if he didn't do something she would succeed in killing someone. A wooden placard hung nailed to a wall next to where he stood, and he tugged it free. The woman aimed into the procession and Lyken started forward quickly, shoving aside members of the crowd. He kept his eyes on the archer as she steadied her bow while he held aloft the makeshift wooden shield. The assassin released her arrow, and Lyken sprinted to intercept it. His goal? Prevent a murder.

Much like a fist pounding against a wall, the arrow thudded into the wooden placard, intercepting a mortal blow to its intended target. Lyken was in the middle of the procession now. He had rushed in, knocking soldiers away, not thinking of the consequences, but to the benefit for one member of the procession. The arrow now stuck in Lyken's placard shield had targeted young Helga's heart.

The crowd stood frozen in shock. They were startled anyone had dared to try to kill Helga, and equally amazed that a stranger had, in fact, saved her life. Lady Helvys' pupils engulfed her eyes, and her normally cream-colored complexion was specter-white.

Helga's father drew his sword and aimed it at Lyken, but with the realization of Lyken's deed, the lord froze in mid-gesture. Helga narrowed her eyes and bared her teeth. Lyken read in those eyes her ingratitude. She didn't need help from a simple-minded peasant. Fearing her response, Lyken dropped the placard, which hit the mud like a light knock on a heavy door.

Another three arrows rained down on the procession, catching one man in the neck and another in the chest. Lyken backed away as Lord Helvys grabbed his wife and daughter and retreated to the castle. "Guards! To us!"

Helga fingered her flail. "Let them come, Father. I shall bathe in their blood tonight."

Lyken turned and ran with Helga's rebuttal ringing in his ears. As he slipped around a corner, he marveled at the audacity of

Helvys' sole heir. Certainly she deserved her ruthless reputation, the sound of her ball-and-chain flail whirring behind him.

Lyken knew he had to put distance between himself and the scene. He should be hailed a hero, but Helga's expression of disdain for his quick thinking told a different story. He had insulted the girl by saving her, and he didn't want to face her wrath.

Finding a place to hunker down was Lyken's foremost concern. No money, no comrades, he'd had to steal his last meal of stale bread when he arrived at Nor. Someone would want to take him back to the castle; his goal was to hide and wait. Eventually, he would have to sneak out of Nor, likely to the Marsh of Wishes, a dangerous place full of witches and snake-like men. Or he could travel south to Exile, the prison town. But tonight? Find a safe haven.

Lyken dashed down long alleys and streets to the east until he came to a place where the rickety dwellings looked as tenuous as houses of cards. He spotted an abandoned, shuttered shop, sandwiched between a nondescript miller's store and a haberdasher establishment with shabby garments in the window. No one occupied the street right now for most people were attending the christening where the royal procession had been headed. Lyken wrenched two boards free in the vacant store and slithered through the opening, wedging the slats back into place.

The only items left in the small location were shattered and burnt pieces of wood, a couple of rusty chisels on the floor in a corner, and an interesting illustration on the wall of a ship's masthead of a serpent. Lyken ignored everything there for the moment and scurried to a dark spot on the edge of the room, crouching down and breathing deeply to calm himself.

He became the huntsman again—his calling in Kingdom. A good hunter had patience, anticipated the moves of his prey, and reacted at exactly the right moment. He steadied his breathing, actively plotting his next move and his route out of Nor.

Within minutes, someone grabbed a board off the window and yanked it free, allowing sunlight to spill into the dusty room. Lyken tensed but fell back on his experience and remained still, out of the light making an inverted triangular shape on the floor. Sometimes while hunting, the situation changed, and he became the target. He found assessing the situation before making a move the wisest choice. Lyken grasped his knife's hilt and focused on the opening as a leopard focuses on a deer.

An arrow sailed through the hole and the point struck the wall not a foot from his shoulder. The archer hadn't intended to kill him but had released the missile to provide cover for a man in black who entered, sword-first, into the abandoned room. The man moved like a cat and slipped inside quickly, slashing his blade in front of him as his eyes adjusted to the darkness. Lyken's knife was no match for the man's broadsword by any means, and his mind raced to the idea of throwing his only weapon. He was a skilled fighter at both close and far distances.

A second arrow cut through the dust motes in the opposite direction and embedded itself into another wall as an additional person entered. This figure was shorter, not half the size of a man. She had no weapons in her hands, but her embroidered cloak and colorful tattoos identified this invader as a magic wielder. Lyken's pulse quickened. He hadn't often squared off against those practiced in the mystical arts and worried he couldn't defeat her.

The archer stuck his head inside the deserted shop last. Lyken caught a glimpse of the young man's fair features: pointed beard, hawk-like nose, sunken cheekbones. The bowman removed another board from the window and inserted his upper body into the opening, readying his weapon.

The fighter with the broadsword spotted Lyken and turned his way. His weapon ready, the large man with gray hair, bushy eyebrows, and a braided beard advanced across the room. While he didn't rush to attack, his movement informed the hunter he wasn't there merely to shake hands. The man grunted at the Kingdom refugee while his short companion, a leprechaun woman, gestured and pointed, pulling magic from the energy in the still room.

When he spoke, the man's accent identified him as a Nor

resident. "Why did you do it?"

He came closer. Lyken waited until the most opportune moment to pull his dagger, though knowing that doing so wouldn't make a difference. Engaging them in conversation was his only option.

"I do not know what you mean."

The braided-beard man squinted at Lyken. "Why did you help her?"

A flame flickered from the tips of the leprechaun's hair. "We had her. Who are you? What have you told them?"

Lyken realized that these three were part of the assassin's crew, likely integral in the distraction. They had tracked him through the streets of Nor, believing he'd had foreknowledge of the plot. Would they accept that he had acted out of instinct? Not likely.

Bradley, I leave this life. I hope to meet you in the next.

His internal friend didn't answer while Lyken unsheathed his knife as the sword came into range. He used the flat side of the blade to push aside the sword's longer and more deadly point and then rushed the fighter. He connected with the man in mid-step— at his attacker's most unbalanced. Lyken's skill caught his opponent at just the right moment, and he threw his arms around the man's waist, positioning braided-beard in the line of sight of the magic wielder. Unfortunately, at the same time, the bowman had a clear shot at him.

The leprechaun shouted, "Stand clear, Nooge."

The man named Nooge ignored her and switched tactics to close combat as green starbursts exploded behind his head, temporarily blinding Lyken. The hunter closed his eyes and used his other senses to engage his adversary. He heard the man's breathing, labored from running across the city, and smelled the man's body odor. Using sound, Lyken judged his challenger's distance. He delivered a blow to Nooge's jaw using his head and it clanked like a stone striking pottery. Success, but he still stood exposed in this space. What had happened to his third enemy, the archer?

Nooge threw Lyken to the floor, and the hunter gasped

when he landed. His sight started to clear as he swept his leg and knocked his opponent off his feet. The man fell hard and cursed as Lyken leapt up and regained his footing. While the green glowing spots faded from view, the hunter assessed his situation. The swordsman rose at the same time Lyken readied himself; the magician had red tips on the ends of her fingers; and the man with a bow had simply vanished.

Lyken knew he had to eliminate Nooge from this battle. He flipped his wrist and threw his dagger at the attacker's neck. His accuracy rarely failed him, and the knife pierced the center of his opponent's throat. The man's eyes bugged out, and he put his hands on the dagger and struggled to free himself. Whether he succeeded or not didn't matter. He was a dead man.

The refugee turned to the magician, forgetting the archer for the moment. The faint hope he'd held out was quickly extinguished as a spell covered him, making him pause before he regained his bearings. Lyken felt crushingly exhausted. Heavy as ship anchors, his legs remained rooted to the floor. His hands shook, and he noticed they were covered with wrinkles and spots. He clutched his chest, which had transformed into a thin, frail structure. Gasping, he released a reedy breath. The magic wielder had grievously aged him.

The leprechaun grinned, but her satisfaction was short lived. An arrow flew across the room and struck the small being in the back of the head, forcing her forward and then down face-first to the floor.

Immediately, the aging process reversed and Lyken inhaled deeply, regaining his strength. A different figure than the archer stood in the opening to the building. Hood covering his head, he entered the room gracefully and surveyed both of Lyken's attackers, kicking the dead leprechaun. As he did, he lowered his hood and the hunter received his second shock in a short period. He was not a he but a she, and he knew her.

The woman resembled many maidens in Kingdom: receding chin, round cheekbones—and abbreviated, dark eyelashes. However, one feature stood out—she had no hair. Her bald pate, her skill with a bow, her presence in Nor all revealed her identity, though Lyken had never met her before.

"Garmine!" he shouted.

Garmine was formerly a Kingdom soldier and a member of an elite team that performed special tasks for the king. Lyken had viewed the painting of the team on the royal palace's gallery wall many times when he had visited, and the artist had done exemplary work capturing Garmine's features. He was shocked when the town crier announced that Garmine had deserted Kingdom for Nor and was to be considered a traitor to the crown.

Garmine didn't acknowledge Lyken but examined the braided-bearded man, flipping him over with her foot. She then addressed Lyken without taking her eyes from the dead man. "I would like to know who you are, and why you have come to Nor. Your fighting style betrays you as a Kingdom resident."

Lyken retrieved his knife and wiped the blood on the dead man's tunic. "My name is unimportant. All that matters is I am being hunted by a bloodthirsty enemy for an act of mercy."

He thought keeping his past shrouded in secrecy to be the best choice. He didn't know if Garmine still had allies in her former country of allegiance, and he didn't want anyone to connect his present life to his past.

Garmine's eyes flitted to him then back to the dead pair on the ground. "Truly, mercy is a crime in Kingdom." She had accepted his response with no further questions, then leaned down and removed a sash from the dead leprechaun's waist. She threw it at Lyken. "Wrap this around your head so only your eyes are revealed and tie it at the end. Lady Helvys herself has ordered me to return with you to the castle."

Lyken had hoped Garmine would let him go for saving Helga's life, and wasn't pleased with the turn of events. But Garmine's accuracy with any weapon was legendary; he knew crossing her would yield him no advantage. He quickly followed her orders and left only his eyes exposed—the rest of his head now covered in a teal cloth.

Garmine said, "Let me take your arm. I shall keep your

identity a secret. Not a word until we reach the castle."

She lifted her hood, hiding her lack of hair, and led him from the abandoned building and down multiple narrow streets until they came to the side of the castle. The lord's house was a multi-towered, plain construct with moss growing rampant over its lower level. The archer, instead of going through the front door, led him to a back entrance, less heavily guarded because of a plank placed across a moat.

Garmine spoke to a sentry for a minute, and eventually the doorkeeper lifted a hand to signal others. Two guards with bows and arrows stepped back from murder holes positioned in an arch above the entrance. Garmine and the hunter proceeded into the castle and down a maze of corridors. Instead of paintings, the wooden planks of ships hung on the walls.

Lyken whispered, "Bradley, how do I escape from this situation?"

Bradley rarely answered, but when he did, his advice was usually sound. This time a voice responded: "Why would Lady Helvys hurt you? You saved her daughter. If you were a Kingdom spy, you would never have saved her."

Bradley gave wise counsel, and his logic calmed the hunter.

They advanced up two different sets of stairs until Garmine led him into a large room with weapons mounted on a wall and an enormous window overlooking the western grounds. For the first time, Garmine smiled and asked him to remove his makeshift mask. "I shall tell Lady Helvys you are here. Relax, my friend without a name. I believe she wants to reward you."

Lyken took a deep breath as Garmine turned around and left by a different door than the one where they had entered. Lyken rocked on his heels, wondering if Lady Helvys would grant him a boon. His needs were simple—a place to work, a modest income, and a chance to remain anonymous. While waiting, he surveyed the weapons on the walls until he heard footsteps approaching. Helga, not Lady Helvys, entered through a massive, studded door, her black braids bouncing as she strode in.

Stiffening while she drew near him, Lyken tried his best to

appear servile. She didn't say a word but stopped two inches away —the top of her head level with his neck. He guessed he was approximately ten years her senior.

Lyken began to bow, but she shook her head. Instead, she examined his arms and legs and lingered a moment on the scar under his jaw, which had never healed after a battle with an animated tree years before. She stepped back, put her hands on her hips, and tipped her head. "You will do."

Helga. Her presence filled him with dread, though she should be thanking him. She was renowned as a conniving devil, as likely to kill you for sport as to let you live. He found his voice. "My lady?" he asked.

Helga moved away from him and walked to the wall, retrieving a broadsword from a bracket. Its hilt was gilded in silver and inlaid with small rubies. She returned and threw him the sword, point downward. "I dislike being saved by anyone. My people may then imagine I am the type who needs saving. To show my strength, I must best you in combat."

Lyken caught the hilt with both hands but kept its point downward. "There is no need, my lady. I am sure you are the more accomplished warrior."

Helga removed a flail with ball-and-chain from the wall and held it high. She also grabbed a short sword as she swung the spiked ball around furiously, and Lyken observed a hardness in her eyes. Suddenly, she screamed and ran at him. Lyken stood still, hoping she would halt before attacking him, but at the last minute he was forced to dodge her. She elbowed him as she adjusted to his countermeasure and aimed her spindly bone into a soft spot under his ribs.

Lyken stumbled away while Helga prepared to launch herself a second time. From a hook on the wall, he grabbed a square shield with Nor's insignia emblazoned on it.

Helga pounced at Lyken like a cat, swinging her flail. He managed to raise the shield at the last minute, and the flail bounced off it. The effort cost him his footing, and he stumbled away.

The spiked ball beat on the shield again and again, metal ringing against metal. Lyken realized she was not simply sparring. If he didn't defend himself, the weapon would hit him at full force—embedding itself deep into his body. He was not going to survive if he only stopped her blows.

Clang. He used his sword to knock the hilt of the flail away. For a moment, she stood open-armed, defenseless. Lyken lowered his head like many trapped deer he had cornered and charged forward. The feral move surprised Helga, and his head connected with her gut. Her leather jacket absorbed most of the blow, but she staggered back.

Lyken had hoped the daring maneuver would impress her. She would respect him and stop the battle, but Helga reacted differently. Her cheeks flushed with indignation. "You shoat! My flail will drip with your blood!"

So much for impressing her.

Helga charged forward, ball spinning, and Lyken eyed the spikes in fear. At the last minute, she swung her sword and the hunter adjusted his shield to intercept it. The edge of the shield met the blade and deflected the blow but at a cost. The force of the attack wrenched Lyken's safeguard from his grip, and it landed on the marble-laid floor.

Helga kicked the shield away, swinging her flail downward in an arc at Lyken's head. He managed to parry with his sword to absorb the blow—but chain and blade hopelessly entangled. She grinned wickedly. He had no shield, no sword, and she was still armed. Lyken stood exposed as Helga stabbed with her blade.

He dodged the blow by less than the width of an apple stem. Hoping to free his weapon from hers, Lyken stood in close proximity to Lord Helvys' daughter. She twisted her sword like a key in a lock and aimed at his gut. This time he wouldn't be able to elude the steel.

"Stop!"

The voice at the door startled the warrior girl, and the sword's tip halted next to Lyken's waist. Her eyes flashed with frustration as she lowered her weapons—a lioness cheated of her meal. In the doorframe stood an elegant lady in a white dress with pearls sewn into the trim and down the arms like a gown on an older bride. Her face was powdered white, and her gray hair braided in two places, hanging on her shoulders.

"Mother," Helga demurred. "We were only sparring."

Garmine appeared behind the Lady of Nor, peeking over her right shoulder, eyes widening. The woman in the white dress folded together her brick-colored gloves. "The graveyard knows too much of your sparring, my daughter. Allow me a private moment with your rescuer."

Helga's lower lip stuck out at her mother's last word. She dropped her flail. "I know your intent. I will stay."

Garmine stepped across the room to Lyken's side. While Helga's attention was focused on her mother, Lyken noticed Garmine's fingers curled around her knife, ready, he thought, to defend him in case Helga disobeyed her mother, which Lyken was afraid she might.

Lady Helvys leaned forward. "By Saint Peter's beard, Helga, you will listen to me. Garmine, escort her out."

"To ensure I will not listen in?" the daughter inquired churlishly.

The lady crossed her arms.

Helga threw her sword to the ground. "As you wish, you saddle-goose!"

Lyken stiffened at the insult, but the lady bore it graciously and eyed her daughter as she left the room. Garmine bowed to the lady and followed Helga out, closing the door behind them. The footsteps of the pair receded until they no longer made a sound, and then Lady Helvys' features softened. Lyken watched her transform from an imposing leader of Nor to a weary parent. She gestured for Lyken to approach her.

Lyken stepped forward and bowed his head. "My lady."

The woman squared her shoulders, restoring the visage of the leader of Nor. "I apologize for my daughter. I am afraid she grows in skill and impertinence equally. You are not hurt?"

Lyken shook his head.

"Good. My foremost purpose is to thank you for protecting her. She is a proud creature and will not submit to the idea she owes anything to anyone. However, I am in your debt. You have saved my beloved daughter."

Beloved? Bradley, did you hear her? "Any gentleman would have done the same."

Lady Helvys' mouth twitched. "You are a foreigner. This statement is either born from a sense of chivalry or ignorance of Nor. On that point, why are you here? Are you a spy for King Shade?"

"Indeed not. I have a powerful adversary in Kingdom—Madame Faye Whisper. I am hiding from her."

"Will she follow you here?"

"Kingdom's citizens know not to cross Nor's boundaries. 'Tis the reason why people seek refuge here."

"True. We have seen an influx of inhabitants of late, thanks to your tyrant," said Lady Helvys. "Would you like to stay and take a vow to Nor?"

Lyken hesitated. In his mind, he asked Bradley what he should do, but the internal voice didn't answer.

"Unsure, are you? If you are not seeking asylum, you must leave forthwith. My husband demands loyalty."

"I would gladly swear my allegiance to Nor. This is not the cause of my concern."

"Is it my daughter?"

"She may kill me if I remain."

Lady Helvys folded her arms. "You shall be safe. In fact, I think you would make an excellent guardian."

Lyken was taken aback. "What do you mean?"

"Despite my daughter's behavior, I believe she respects you. She would not have attacked you, otherwise. And the fact you lasted so long in combat with her demonstrates your skill."

"She will resent me for saving her. You said so yourself."

"Helga resents everyone and trusts no one. The fact she respects you works in your favor. I will have the guards escort you to a private room and provide a meal. At the end of the repast, I expect an answer."

The Lady of Nor turned on her heel and exited. Two guards entered after she left and ushered Lyken to a nearby room. A few minutes later, a guard served him a dish of well-cooked mutton and a generous chunk of bread.

After eating, he stood at the window and surveyed Nor, a bustling wood and stone city. Merchants hung a variety of fish at many of the stalls. A stave church sat surrounded by elegant two-story houses, none higher than the steeple of the holy place. Horses clip-clopped down streets, people hailed each other in passing, wagons carrying autumn's bounty rumbled over holes in the dirt roads. Lyken reflected that this was what a royal city should ideally be, nothing like the morose, submissive central town of Kingdom.

The door opened, and Garmine filed in. Lyken bowed to her, and she acknowledged the greeting, joining him at the window. He stepped back to allow her a view of the landscape. Then she, too, focused on the courtyard below, squinting in the sunshine. "Will you stay?"

"If I do, Helga will kill me."

Casting a sidelong glance at Lyken, Garmine gestured, keeping her eyes downward. He went to her again at the window. Below stood Helga, a scarecrow her only companion. She swung her flail in a circle in front of the simulacrum.

Garmine scratched behind her ear. "The king of Kingdom is corrupt. His evil proclamation killed Maydayla, my best friend. She and all of my closest companions, my family, slaughtered by his idiotic rule for no reason at all."

Helga attacked the scarecrow suddenly, the flail flashing and then sinking into the tan clothes of the straw man. The weapon entered its chest and she yanked it back, ripping out handfuls of straw, a light wind scattering the dry stuffing of the mannequin. Lyken tensed while considering what the spiked ball would do to a human being.

Garmine watched the act of violence without reaction. "Kingdom's only chance is if Nor invades, and her leaders sit on

Kingdom's throne. We cannot hope for children's stories of benevolent queens rising from the peasants to come true. We must subdue the giants, march to the castle, and depose the king."

Helga swung her flail in a wide arc, neatly cutting the scarecrow in two, the halves falling to the ground in different directions.

Garmine brushed her fingers over her knife hilt. "We need good fighters to accomplish an invasion of Kingdom, men like you. If you guard Helga, you could influence her to become a woman we want to follow."

Lyken chose his words carefully. "She is an impudent, violent, and possibly heartless brat, not a lady. I would have no influence on her."

Below, Helga looked over her shoulder at the setting of the sun. She appeared to convulse and ran for the door of the castle. Garmine pressed her fingertips on the ledge. "Rumors in this castle, Lyken, suggest that Helga has more to her than meets the eye. Become her guard. She took out her frustration on the scarecrow. She will no longer bother you. Stay with us. We will protect you here, and you will protect us in return."

Garmine nodded to him and then left the room. Lyken remained at the window and joined his hands behind his back. The setting sun's rays colored the roofs of Nor, turning the turrets and tiles a bright shade of gold. His heart longed for the serenity of the scene below.

"Am I here to stay, Bradley?" The girl was talented though deadly. Could he survive long enough to train her?

Bradley seemed to acquiesce, though perhaps the answer came from Lyken. And at that moment, Lyken made his decision and adopted Nor as his city.

Cottage

ABANDONED: A RETELLING

"Abandoned."

The beggar whispered the word as if telling herself a secret too horrible to speak aloud. Eyes downcast, she repeated the word, not merely mouthing it but tasting it, as one might rotten fruit or curdled milk. She reclined at the side of the dirt path in front of a small grove of trees, a child not much older than fourteen, fifteen at most.

Pulling back raven-black locks twisted with clumps of dirt, she rubbed her skin, which stretched thin across her starving face—a mask of death. She lay on her side cushioned by her outstretched arm, her head resting on the crook of her elbow. Dust and dirt marred her skin, with only thin lines of a lighter color running down her cheeks, marking her tear tracks.

The dwarf named Deer had spotted the damsel at the side

of the road and stared while the rest of his brothers simply ignored her. They had avoided all the beggars on their way, trying to arrive at the monastery before nightfall. Their destination, Saint Cuthbert the Generous, lay across the steppes within the Plains of Isolation. They had no time for the homeless on their annual pilgrimage to worship their creator and pay their tribute. As the youngest, at a mere twenty years of life, Deer had followed their example and had kept his focus bent on the dirt trail.

But this girl drew his attention, an inner voice urging him to examine the indigent child. He alone locked eyes with her and considered her plight, recognizing her desperation. Though she caught his attention, the homeless girl's eyes remained hazy and held no hope for an offering.

The dwarfs advanced across the terrain, Deer a little slower than the others, but leaving behind the supplicant on their journey to the monastery, nonetheless. Deer's brother Squirrel chatted about catching a glimpse of Magdala the Priestess, and his other brother Hedgehog responded that Magdala's latest actions risked King Shade's ire. Deer ignored them, his thoughts focused on the teenager they had left behind.

Abandoned.

Deer recognized her hopeless situation, but thought she'd likely brought it on herself. Most beggars were swindlers, thieves, or pickpockets, hoping to score with pilgrims headed for the holy site. Perhaps she was an excellent actress who played on the emotions of the virtuous. She would rely on their charity and then escape in the middle of the night with their riches. Riches? What riches? Gads, would she be disappointed if she stole from them.

Yet the steady, internal voice remained, urging him to turn around and look again. Something drew him to the vagrant, but a thought countered these impulses. "She will steal your lifestyle. She may be a tramp and infect ye and your brothers with ignominious diseases."

Deer ceased his march to the monastery. Why not stop and give the beggar a few coins? They had enough to spare. What held him back?

"She is not worth it."

He said this aloud, and his family halted and turned to him. Bull, the oldest and strongest of his brood, rubbed his chin. "Magdala is certainly worth seeing, Deer."

Deer blinked, hardly listening to his brother. Why had he spoken his thought aloud? Why was he suspicious of the girl? Nothing about her warranted his avoidance of her.

The brothers stood and waited for him to resume their journey. Instead, he turned around, half-expecting the person at the side of the road to be gone. Hoping, even. Her absence would make his decision easier. Yet she reclined in the same location, in the same position, hand outstretched, wishing for a little charity.

His brother Fox adjusted the bag on his shoulder. "What troubles ye, young'un?"

Deer blinked and responded as if mesmerized. "We have to help her."

His brothers eyed each other, concern and impatience predominant in their eyebrows and the turn of their mouths. Fox stepped forward. "Help who? Magdala?"

Deer shook his head and pointed to the girl behind them. "Her."

The others of his family of pilgrims followed his finger to the prone child at the side of the road. They did not avert their eyes from her now, for her back was to them. They observed her, attempting to understand their brother's insistence on his charitable deed. His sibling Hedgehog reached for him. "Come along now, Deer. She is just a beggar girl. We have passed dozens and will cross dozens more on our way."

He avoided Hedgehog's hand. "We need to help her."

The group regarded each other without addressing Deer at first. Fox grimaced. "Why her?"

"She is abandoned."

Bull snorted and kicked at the dirt. "Unfortunately, my young brother, they are all abandoned. I will tell ye what. I have an excess coin I planned to spend at the campground tonight. Ye may have it. The next beggar we pass, ye may give it to them."

Deer's eyes remained still, unblinking. "We are not going on the pilgrimage."

Responses, all spoken at once.

"What are ye talking about?"

"Of course we are."

"Stop this foolishness."

Turtle slowly moved forward and placed his hand on his younger brother's slender shoulder. "Come along. The day passes, and we would be wise to arrive at the campsite before nightfall."

Deer shook him off. "No. If ye want to go on without me, go on, but I am returning to help that girl."

Deer spun on his heel and marched toward the beggar as his brothers called after him. He wondered if they would restrain him and drag him on their way, but they weren't the types to bully him around. Normally, they all got along and shared responsibility for maintaining their cottage or working in the mines. Oh, they played tricks on one another and tweaked each other about how they resembled the animals they were named after, but the brothers were loyal to each member of the family, never dismissing a sibling's concern.

The other six hurried to catch up to Deer, falling in step behind him. Fox walked with him shoulder to shoulder. "Listen, brother. We shall give her bread and water, enough to sustain her for half a day, and then we shall march double-time to our destination."

Confidence filled Deer with every step he took. "I would like to hear her story."

"Oh, for heaven's sake," Bull murmured, stomping instead of walking. "This fuss about an ordinary human, no less. It would be one thing if she were a dwarf, but she may be in league with the tax collectors."

Fox touched the white tuft on his chin. "She is half-starved, Bull. Not a tax collector."

Deer pulled ahead and stopped before the reclining maiden. Head inches from his dusty and worn-down black boots, she rolled over to look up at him. Fear flashed in her pupils, and she struggled to push herself away. To his surprise, she acted more frightened of him than he of her. Strange for someone to ask for charity and then run away.

"Young lady, do ye seek something to eat?" His tone was gentle and inviting.

She shook her head at first, and he noticed her beauty then. Not comparable to a dwarven maiden, certainly, but for a human, her features were balanced and exquisite. The mud, dust, and hunger hid her delicately carved cheeks, petite nose, heart-shaped lips.

The brothers gathered around the girl in a semicircle. To Deer, the young lady didn't at all resemble a charlatan ready to take them for their riches. He knew Fox could always spot a ruse, and he noticed his brother touched his chin with growing interest.

The sight of seven of them together served to frighten her further, Deer observed. The girl tried to push herself away. Deer now saw the situation from her point of view. Seven men surrounding a weak and helpless child: he with his fuzzy, brown crewcut; Fox with his white tuft of a beard; and Bull! Bull, stout and broad-shouldered, frightened most human men. Indeed, a skittish dwarf himself would tremble before the animal-featured pilgrims.

Deer crouched down and extended his hand. "Please, we do not mean to harm ye."

"Ye owe us nothing in return," said Turtle. "If such is the cause of your concern."

Deer appreciated his brother's sagacity and kept his arm steady and palm open. He extended his other hand to Rabbit, the keeper of their rations. "Give me some bread."

The girl shrunk back into herself like a frightened animal. Ironically, she reminded Deer of a deer. Maybe their similar nature connected the two of them, but he thought something else urged him to help her.

Rabbit handed him bread, and Deer pushed it toward the maiden. "Please."

She regarded each in turn, her eyes filled with trepidation while she took short breaths. She didn't snatch the bread but broke off a piece and popped it into her mouth, chewing quickly. Fox retrieved a tin cup from a sack then passed it to Rabbit, and the white-haired man sloshed water from the skin to the container.

Still trembling, the girl accepted the container and drank from it, but her irises remained enlarged and focused on them. A drop of water escaped the side of her mouth and she took her index finger from her other hand and caught it. As she pulled away from the cup, she sucked the finger, consuming every drop.

Fox crouched to her line of sight. "What is your name, child?"

Her nostrils flared, not in anger, but alarm. "Gretal."

Deer recognized the lie, and why not? Why trust seven strangers even if they gave her food? Names were important. Evil wizards cast serious curses with but a name. Arms at his side, palms outward, he declared, "I am Deer."

"Dear?"

The way she said it, he knew she didn't refer to the animal. Though he had short, brown hair like fur and a jumpy way about him, she hadn't connected him with his mammal namesake. When he met other people, they observed him and inclined their heads, equating him with the timid beasts.

But not her.

He responded as softly as a feather tickling a nose. "Like the animal in a forest."

"Oh." Her voice was high. Chirpy.

He offered her the rest of the bread. "Please, eat it all."

She took the bread and ate another piece. "You are too kind. Normally, I would not ask for so much, but I am near famished."

Deer detected no deception in her voice or manner, so he decided what to do next right there. He stood while she ate and gestured to his brothers to step away. "A word?"

The siblings followed their brother's lead and walked

away from the starving girl then huddled together. The young-est dwarf kept his attention on the maiden as he whispered, "We should take her home."

An absolute silence—one in which a dandelion seed land-ing on the ground could've been heard—met his suggestion. Even-tually Bull found his voice. "Deer, are ye touched by madness?"

"Her hands are not calloused, which indicates a woman of some means. Her accent betrays her as a resident from across the river. Her feet are ragged. She has been running from someone but is at the end of her strength."

Rabbit's mouth twitched. "So we give her sustenance and then set her on her way."

Deer flinched at the suggestion. "When I first noticed her, I thought I heard a voice warding me away. 'Tis like she is under a spell, keeping people from her. Did ye hear it?"

Their silence was all the answer he needed.

"But some other force, deeper inside me, drew me to her. She is an innocent. Powerful magic repels people away from her."

"All the more reason not to assist her," said Bull.

Deer straightened his shoulders. "No. We should help her. Why go on this pilgrimage if we refuse to help the poorest of the poor? She is no stronger than any of us, full belly or not."

"Brother, consider this." Rabbit lowered his voice. "A young girl in a house with seven, grown men. We are honorable dwarfs and have no other intentions than to help her, but what do ye think people will say? Her parents could find her and claim we kidnapped her. Make wild accusations about us. We have few friends in the community. We may end up in a dungeon for the rest of our lives."

Deer hadn't thought about what the neighbors would think of their lodging a female without a guardian, but leave it to his vain brother to come to that conclusion. He was grateful Rab-bit had brought it forward, however. "If our reasons are pure, we should do what is right, no matter how it looks."

Fox rubbed his cheek with the back of his fingers. "Our kind and humans do not mix. I do not recall a friendship between the

two since we dwarfs stepped away from King Shade's proclam-
ations."

Turtle extended his neck. "Indeed. The smooth, clean-
shaven chin of human women is unappealing."

Deer observed the maiden across the field. "I want to help
her. Ye may proceed onward to the monastery, but I want to give
her enough food and drink to accompany me to our cottage."

Bull's shoulders sagged, Rabbit shifted from foot to foot,
and Turtle retracted his head. He read their body language while
they considered his proposal. As the youngest brother, Deer had
always been submissive, not rebellious, but they sensed his resolve on this course of action and knew it must be important to
him.

Fox nudged Deer's shoulder. "Fair enough. Let us see if the
young lady will allow us to escort her back to our house."

Deer spent ten minutes convincing her to return with
them to their cottage. Gretal, as she called herself, eventually relinquished and agreed to accompany the dwarfs to their home in
the hills surrounding the mountains of Grok's Teeth. Despite her
desperate situation, her answers to their questions were evasive
at first, not giving them any information about her current situation. While on the path to their home, they introduced themselves one by one, and the beggar regarded them with her eyes
lowered. "If I may ask, did you name yourselves after your animal
likenesses?"

Bull lowered his head. "No. Our mother named us. 'Tis a
long story."

Rabbit hunched into himself. "And not interesting at all."

The girl pressed her lips together, and Deer sensed she
wanted to know their family history. He cleared his throat. "Our
mother broke a bargain with a witch who cursed her to give birth
to children who looked like beasts. An unimaginative woman,
she named us after the animals we resemble. I know I am slen-

der for a dwarf and long-limbed with pointed, small ears. Hence, Deer."

The brothers hung their heads. Gretal seemed to notice their reaction to the story and tapped her fingers together. "Certainly you should not be blamed for your mother's curse. Do not be ashamed of yourselves. If others look down on you, the fault lies with them, not you."

Deer observed their companion with newfound interest. Their community had chastised them all their lives and made remarks behind their backs. They had no voice, no advocate in the world. Gratitude shone in the eyes of his brothers. Deer, as the youngest, often made mistakes, but he stood tall in his decision to help the beggar girl despite his brothers' reluctance.

The dwarfs and the maiden swapped stories of their encounters with wildlife. Gretal claimed shy animals overcame their reticence with her and approached, allowing her to caress them. Wildlife also ignored or accompanied the brothers without fear. Gretal told them of cranky vultures who did her bidding, and then Turtle described a tortoise with a cracked shell that he had adopted. Both the girl and the dwarfs shared stories of their infrequent glimpses of unicorns.

The longer they traveled together, the more the maiden and the dwarfs enjoyed each other's company. At sunset, they approached the men's home, and Gretal stopped and clapped her hands with delight at the sight of it. The triangular-shaped wooden cottage, sturdy but small, had the front door at one of its points. Large enough to house the seven men, the dwelling boasted sleeping arrangements in an open loft, and a kitchen and dining room on the lower floor.

Gretal entered and proclaimed the interior charming with such enthusiasm that the dwarfs' chests swelled with pride. They had built the cottage from three large oak trees with the furniture made of the same sturdy material. The tables and chairs were cut and shaped as if they had grown out of the ground. The knotholes and wood tracks lined up among the chairs and tables, and the dwarfs left small branches on the furniture to give the impression their cabin had grown inside of a tree.

Gretal proclaimed she would be on her way in the morning, but the dwarfs, gentlemen to their core, urged her to stay. Their journey to their home with her had solidified a familial relationship. She, their long-lost sister, gentle cousin, outcast sibling, deserved their best accommodations. They relinquished the best bed in the loft to her. She demurred, proclaiming she would sleep on the floor, but they insisted and wouldn't listen to her protests. They went so far as to carry the rest of the beds from the loft to the ground floor so that she had sole use of the higher level.

The next day, after a hearty breakfast, Deer retrieved a kindly neighbor named Nelda. Nelda, a slim dwarven woman with a brown beard, mended Gretal's clothes while the dwarf's guest took a second bath. While their lodger scrubbed herself in the tub behind the cottage, Nelda brushed the girl's hair to remove the mud and tangles.

When Gretal returned to the cottage at last, the dwarfs all held their breath. No human girl compared to the lovely maiden they now beheld in their doorway. After his initial shock at her transformation, Deer bowed and gestured for her to enter, and she blushed and went inside.

In the main room, Gretal spun around and rubbed her hands together, aware of their astonishment. "You are all too considerate. I cannot repay you. I am sure your mother would be proud of the men you have become."

Bull grunted. "Ha. Little ye know of our mother."

"She must have been the very honey of sweetness."

Hedgehog puffed out his chest. "Ye did not know our mother. We were ostracized because of our nature. People picked on us, but we refused to return such rudeness to them. We, the Animal Brothers, will not give them what they want. A reaction."

"We took an oath to treat evil with kindness," Deer said. "Not that it has done us any good."

Gretal sat down. "I am sorry I was hesitant to accept your invitation. I once met a cruel dwarf. My friend and I did him multiple favors and all he did was complain about us."

The girl tried to excuse herself so she might be on her way, but the dwarf siblings insisted she stay. Deer beamed with pride at his brothers who treated her like royalty. They all chatted and visited the rest of the morning and afternoon.

The following day, the brethren picked up their tools and excused themselves to go to the mine. When Gretal said she'd leave, the dwarfs insisted she remain as their guest. She claimed she had imposed on their hospitality too long, but Deer argued with her, saying the first thing he ever regretted. "If ye feel ye are an imposition, then make us a light supper. Ye do not need to cook for us, but if it will keep ye here, we shall appreciate it."

"I am not much of a chef," she replied.

Bull picked up a miner's pike. "I am sure ye are wonderful at it."

The dwarfs made their living extracting precious jewels and metals from the mountains of Grok's Teeth. They promised to be home well before sundown, and Gretal said she would not leave the cottage in the meantime.

When they returned, Gretal had made a stew for the brothers. Though it smelled foul, they started eating and forced down their first spoonful. After Gretal slurped her portion, she covered her mouth and ran for the door. With her away, the dwarfs emptied their bowls out the back window, deeming it not esculent, and each took a hunk of bread for dinner.

As the weeks progressed, Gretal went on walks with her newfound friends, sometimes in groups but often one on one. Deer walked with her the most, and the mysterious connection between them persisted.

Five months after the maiden came to live with them, the dwarfs went off to the mine in their usual routine. After eight hours of labor, Deer stopped pushing a wheelbarrow while hauling away a load of rocks. His ears twitched, and he stood still. He shuddered with...anticipation? No. Dread! The rocks knocked against each other as the wheelbarrow rattled in his hands.

Noticing the disturbance, Fox wiped dirt from his face. "What is it, brother?"

Deer dropped the wheelbarrow handles. "I fear for our maiden. Something is amiss."

Fox regarded him, tucking back his head. "We still have two hours of work."

Yet Deer couldn't explain his heightened anxiety to his brother. More than anything, he wanted to run home to the cottage. "I wish to leave."

Fox leaned on his pick. "Ye worry too much, but ye may go. Make sure to start dinner. Do not let her prepare our meal again." He cupped his hands to call "or ever!"

Deer ignored Fox's request and sped off homeward. He called for Gretal as he sprinted toward their wooden hideaway, but she didn't answer. Short of breath, he rushed into the cottage and spied the maiden prone on the floor. He crouched down and examined her, noticing she wasn't breathing. Her pale complexion had lightened to be as white as a moth's wing.

The dwarf surveyed his lodger for wounds and a corset caught his eye. When they had set out for work this morning, Gretal hadn't been wearing a corset, and Deer noticed now how it restricted her waist. He grabbed for the laces and tried to loosen them, but they resisted. Someone had enchanted the strings to slip from his grasp.

In a panic, Deer drew his knife and slipped the edge under the lace. As he went to cut it, his fingers shook and he plunged the knife into Gretal's side. He cursed his clumsiness, withdrew the knife, and snipped one of the laces. The corset loosened and he mumbled a prayer. Suddenly, the maiden took a long breath, sucking in a deep lungful of air. Deer fell back on his bottom and wiped his brow.

He helped her to her feet and escorted her to a bed on the ground floor. She sat on it, and held her head while Deer steadied her with a hand on her back. "What happened, Gretal?"

When she caught her breath enough to speak, she said, "An

old peddler lady called on your household. She said she had items for me as well, showed me a beautiful corset, and claimed I would look exquisite with it on. She convinced me to slip into it but then pulled it too tight. I should have known, vain thing that I am, it was a trick."

The youngest dwarf glared at the article of clothing on the floor, regarding it as he would a dead scorpion. "But who would want to trick ye? Who would want to do ye harm?"

Gretal's eyes darted to him, then away. "'Tis time I tell you the truth when your brothers come home."

The brothers returned a couple of hours later, and Deer related the entire episode to them. Gretal sat at the end of the table and folded her hands on the wood between two upright branches. "You deserve to know the truth. I am the daughter of a rich farmer, and my real name is Snow White Whisper," she began. "My mother raised me at first with the love of a parent, but an evil man appeared many seasons past and sold her cursed trinkets, turning her against me. The final object he peddled, a mirror, consumed her attention and smothered her charity. For the last couple of years, she has beaten and imprisoned me."

The dwarfs all exclaimed, and Snow White waited until they had quieted down before she continued. "Her treatment of me grew worse and worse until she ordered our hunter to take me into the forest. She wanted him to murder me, but he took pity on me instead and released me. I fled over the river where a troll accosted me. Because I could not pay the levy, he threw me into the forest. I thought myself dead but managed to make my way to the side of the road where you found me."

Deer asked, "Do ye think the old woman who sold ye the corset was a friend of your mother's?"

"No." She gritted her teeth. "I think she *was* my mother. She has magic items that allow her to disguise herself, but I did not think she would find me here."

The dwarfs all mumbled to each other.

"I am sure now that you will want me to leave," said Snow White. "I will not endanger your lives. I thank you for your patient courtesy, but I must be on my way."

"No," said the youngest dwarf without hesitation. He took her hand. "Ye are our lady."

"Indeed," asserted Bull, and the others all nodded in unison. Their eyes showed their decision. They didn't need to gather or discuss it. They would not make the mistake of parting from the beggar girl again.

Deer squeezed her lily-white palm. "Ye must stay here. Humans avoid the company of our sort. We will alert all our neighbors of spiteful witches and keep an eye on the house. Ye will be safe here."

Tears wetted Snow White's eyelashes. "Please, my mother is not sane."

Fox folded his hands. "All the more reason for ye to remain. Leave, and she will have ye alone. Stay with us, and we will protect ye."

Hedgehog wrinkled his nose. "Please stay, my lady."

Snow White put her hands deep into her hair, pulling on it while contemplating their offer. "I cannot!"

"Where would ye go safer than here?" asked Turtle. "Here, ye have a chance. Here, ye have friends."

Deer interrupted her protest. "Here, ye have family."

His declaration shattered her resolve. "All right. For me to part with you would have been hard, and perhaps she thinks me dead now and shall leave me alone."

Exhausted, Snow White retired to bed early. After her snores drifted down from the loft and the men started to prepare their beds, Turtle made an offhand remark. "Lucky ye came when ye did, or she may have died."

Deer fluffed a pillow. "'Twas strange. She said her mother came to her around noon. Yet I arrived hours later. How did she remain alive for so long? She was not breathing when I arrived."

"The child must have gotten the time wrong," replied his deep-voiced brother.

Deer moved to the lantern and blew out the light. He padded back to his bed and thought about his brother's last remark.

Snow White was trusting and gullible but not a ninny. He didn't believe she lost track of the time.

The next day, the dwarfs decided one brother would stay at the cottage while the rest went off to work. Guarding her reduced their income, of course, and Snow White urged the brother —Bull in this case—to join his family, but he ignored her protests.

A dwarven brother stayed with Snow White every day for a week, a different brother for each day, until the last, Deer, told her they had to leave her alone the next day. Snow White assured him of her safety with a wave of her hand. Though the two of them had enjoyed the day together, she had known the other six had worked extra hard to make up for lost time, and she obviously worried how much she'd inconvenienced them.

After the overcooked and under-seasoned dinner of quail Snow White had prepared, the brothers addressed her. Fox set down his fork, his plate still half full. "Snow White, promise us ye will not talk to strangers."

Snow White's shoulders went down and her mouth pressed into a thin, white line—a trick given her ruby lips. "Do you think I am a young girl?"

The dwarfs looked at each other. Turtle croaked, "Actually, ye are."

Her eyes rolled around. "Uh. Once I am fifteen, I shall not be treated this way. Kingdom has had queens younger than my age."

Intolerant of her indignation, Deer warned, "Snow White, we are trying to protect ye."

She shrank a little from his admonition. "Yes, my friends. I will not talk to strangers even if they promise me all the gold within Grok's mountains. If they enter without my permission, I shall retreat through the back door and lead them into the pit you have dug today."

Every dwarf scowled but they trusted their lady, and they agreed to leave her alone the next morning.

Three-quarters through the next day, Deer sprang up from sifting the rocks the miners had pulverized and shook his head. The same sense of anxiety he'd felt on the day Snow White's mother had strangled her with the corset returned to him. His nose twitched, and like the animal whose name he bore, he smelled oily smoke and fecund moss wafting through the air—the scent of danger. His head throbbed, and his mouth went dry. Setting down his sifter, he called to his brothers. "I must go to our lady. I fear for her. Again."

Deer sprinted off, and his family stopped their work, gathered their tools, and followed behind. He had a sizeable head start on his brothers, and when he arrived, the sun rested on the horizon, casting the cottage in an ochre-red glow.

Heart thumping, Deer called to Snow White when he approached. No one replied as his legs carried him across the field to his front door, and he burst through, knocking the portal off its hinges, and discovered his lady on the floor.

He first thought she had fallen to the ground, so he bent down to scoop her up and place her on the bed. His thin arms wrapped around her and lifted her. Though the weakest of the brothers, Deer had little trouble carrying the dandelion puff of a girl. He noticed her pallid face and lips that formed an ominous blue line. He had seen these symptoms before in others while down in the mines. Poisonous creatures roamed the depths of Grok's Teeth and the blue tinge to her lips made his pulse race. Toxin!

After he set her down, he examined her for any puncture wounds and found multiple on the top of her scalp. Little pools of dried blood stuck to her dark locks, and Deer used his coarse index fingernail to reopen the wounds. He placed his mouth on the first hole and sucked the blood from the slits he had created. He turned his head away from her, spat, and repeated the process. Two, three, ten times, over and over, he sucked and spat. Then he paused to check on his lady. With a jerk, Snow White inhaled a deep breath.

Deer stepped back, astonished and amazed, brushing his

tongue on his teeth to remove the hair in his mouth. Snow White's eyes flitted and then opened. Spying Deer, she focused and then sat up, alarmed. "She was not Nelda!"

Her exclamation helped him put the pieces together. Snow White wouldn't have talked to a stranger, but she trusted Nelda who had helped her when she had first arrived. Pushing aside the thought she should be dead, Deer gripped Snow White's hand as tears stung his eyes with gratitude. Snow White placed her other hand on top of his and squeezed. When he released a long breath of relief, an azalea-hued blush blossomed in Snow White's cheeks.

The other brothers' voices rang in the distance. Maybe she would listen to his warnings the next time. He thought of a question he wanted to ask her before the others arrived. "When did she trick ye?"

"Midday," Snow White replied.

Deer pointed out the window at the gathering dusk. "Tell them it happened only minutes ago."

The brothers charged inside, rushing in like tumbling acrobats, pushing their siblings in front further into the cottage. Snow White put a hand on her chest and her expression sparkled with delight at their arrival. Deer explained how he had found her, and they gasped at his description of her condition. They surrounded her, each taking turns to hold her hand. She explained what had happened.

"Nelda arrived at...sundown. It was not her, of course." Snow White tensed her shoulders. "Mother! She offered to brush my hair with a beautiful comb. Oh, I should have known. At first, she brushed out the tangles but then she drove the teeth of the comb into my head and the world started to spin."

Fox pointed at the loft and to her bed. "Ye should rest."

A small smile brushed her lips. "I will make dinner."

They all protested, and Deer knew they used the pretense of the attack to avoid another one of her awful meals. Bull and Hedgehog prepared supper, instead, as they urged her to remain in the small bed.

"Nonsense. I am fine," she said.

Deer offered his arm. "Let us take a walk then. Only us."

Snow White agreed, and he helped her to her feet. Her face turned the color of a robin's breast as he escorted her to the door. They exited and slipped out into the early evening—the night music of cicadas and bees surrounding them.

With the cottage in the distance, Deer struggled to find the words to say to her. Should he scold her for not following their instructions? Should he tell her how grateful he was she was alive? Or should he broach the third subject, the topic that bothered him? How had she survived?

Snow White clasped her hands together at her waist. "Thank you again for saving me. I cannot ever repay what I owe you."

"I would never seek reparation."

Snow White breathed deeply. "Perhaps a kiss?"

Deer sucked the air between his teeth and Snow White misstepped and caught herself. "I meant...I know lip kisses are reserved only for those intending to marry. I did not mean..."

Deer smirked at her loss for words. "Ye meant if ye kissed me on the top of the head, would I be insulted because of my height? If I were human, would ye kiss me on my scalp? I have a more important question for ye."

Snow White waved an insect away from her nose. "Why did I not die?"

"Indeed."

Snow White looked into the night sky. "I am different from other people. Although I experience pain like everyone else, death never follows it."

Deer didn't push her for an explanation. He wondered for a moment if she might be a zombie. Her lily-white skin would support the theory, but he hadn't ever heard of a zombie with their wits about them.

Snow White focused on their path. "I never knew about my ability to escape death until the troll threw me against a tree when I could not pay his tax. I did not describe everything that happened. He meant to kill me. He lifted me like a doll and hurled me against a sturdy oak. I am certain my back broke before my head hit the ground. I should have been dead."

"But ye walked away?" he asked.

"I was unconscious," Snow White replied. "I awoke near the end of the night, writhing in pain, but it lessened as the sun rose. The troll had left, and my body healed. Midmorning, I managed to rise to my feet and stumble into the shelter of the woods where I recovered for the remainder of the day."

Deer stopped short. Snow White turned toward him. "I am not lying."

He replied, "I believe ye. The corset, my hastiness with the knife, the poison all prove it. Ye cannot die."

The fair maiden grabbed a fold in her white skirt and twisted it. "I believe I am capable of dying. I am certain I was on the edge of starving to death if you had not come along. I think..." She peered beyond him for a moment. "I think people can harm me but not kill me. I am not, however, immune to the natural ways of death. If lightning were to strike me right now, I am certain I would die."

Deer took her hands. "Whatever your ability, I will not rely on it. I will guard ye with my life."

"I must go. She knows where I live and will not stop."

"Every time she fails, she wastes one more of her tricks. We shall use code words so that ye will know whether it is someone ye may trust."

Snow White smacked her lips. "Deer, I have inconvenienced all of you for too long."

"On the cheek."

Snow White shook her head, puzzled. "What do you mean? Is 'on the cheek' a dwarven saying? We humans say I have put you out on your ear."

"If ye want to thank a dwarf, a peck on the cheek is the best way to show it."

He recognized when she slumped her shoulders that he had won the argument of whether she would stay or go. She would remain. She leaned down and gave him a kiss on his right cheek.

Days passed. Snow White wrote letters to her friend miles away, whiling away the time. To keep her friend safe, she would only call her "the woman in red." She added, "You may trust her. Only her."

"But she might be your mother in disguise," protested Hedgehog.

Snow White lifted her chin. "My mother knows better than to disguise herself as my best friend. I would see through it immediately."

The dwarfs developed a routine that, at first, insulted Snow White but became a game. They would tell her not to trust anyone before they left and then add an "even if she offers you..." At first, they finished the sentence with a corset or a comb, and Snow White stomped her foot. "What sort of a village idiot do you think I am?" So they changed the offering to different items.

"Even if she offers ye an elixir of life?"

"Even if she offers ye a pair of glass slippers?"

"Even if she offers ye a proclamation that the king himself is seeking your hand in marriage?"

And Snow White would answer each one with an equally ridiculous statement.

"What would I do with an elixir of life? I am already living."

"Glass slippers sound too fragile to walk on."

"Me? A queen? Can you imagine?"

One day, during Rabbit's turn, he fumbled for a clever turn of phrase. The others eyed him, impatient to get to work, as he stuttered. "Even if she...offers..." His attention fell on a grove of fruit trees out the back window. "Even if she offers ye a pear?"

Snow White shuddered. "I do not care for pears. Someone once threw a pear at me. I prefer apples."

The dwarfs, done with their routine, hoisted their sacks over their shoulders and marched off. Snow White remained at the window as she did every morning, and the youngest dwarf turned and walked backward a few steps. He raised his hand and she mimicked his wave.

In the mine, Deer took his normal position of sifting through the fine rubble, examining it for traces of precious metals. If they found a vein of raw iron ore, they could sell it to the blacksmith for a hefty price. Deer shuffled the box side to side, his thoughts elsewhere, when the small hairs on his arm stood up straight. He rose to his feet and shouted for his brothers. "I must go."

He started off and ran through the mine. Fox and Squirrel yelled with alarm as he made his way down the tunnel. He didn't make it far. Hands made of stone emerged from the cavern walls, extending from the rock. Arms grew from the stone and grabbed his body. The appendages pulled him into an alcove in the darkness and covered his mouth. Deer's brothers passed without noticing him, and the stone hands muffled his cries. The force of the supernatural arms pressed him against the rock wall, and he found he couldn't fill his lungs with air. What sorcery held him, and why?

Without warning, a circle in midair appeared before the youngest dwarf and made a window to another location. He spied Snow White standing in the interior of his cottage. Next to her, a fiercely beautiful woman gripped her arm. The woman's countenance resembled frozen perfection. She had an accentuated jawbone and a pert nose, but a terrible expression marred her features. Deer thought her equally beautiful to Snow White, but her cruel physiognomy elevated Snow White to "the fairest."

Snow White's eyes widened, and Deer realized she could see him in the same way he saw her. Her mouth dropped open as he struggled against his fetters, groaning from the crushing force of the stone arms. She voiced only one word. "No!"

"Yes, my daughter." The cruel mother reached outside of the border of the circle to reveal a succulent apple on top of her palm, half of it a shiny, sparkling red—the other half, mossy green. Someone had taken a bite from the red side and left the green side untouched. "Eat it, now, or I shall crush this one's bones into the wall! And then the remaining six!"

Tears dripped off Snow White's face. "No, I beg of you."

"You know me, Coal. Do as I say and I will spare them!"

Snow White's trembling hand reached for the apple. She took it from her mother and turned the green side to her mouth. Tears ran down her face as she said, "I love you all. Tell them, Dear. I love you." Again, the way she spoke the word, he knew she hadn't referenced the animal. Deer strained against his granite bonds.

Snow White bit into the apple.

They found her on the floor, the poisoned apple inches from her hand. Her skin, paler than the moon, displayed not death's peace but resignation. Deer again tried to suck the poison from her, cutting the side of her neck, and sucking on the wound. To his dismay, her blood wouldn't flow from the opening. Though he tried for ten minutes, his efforts failed to revive her, and Bull dragged him away or he might've continued all night.

The dwarfs stood around her, heads lowered. Turtle's head shrank into his shirt. "This is not right. A pure heart is not rewarded with death."

"'Tis a simple-minded notion, Turtle." Fox wiped at his forehead. "Kingdom is not the land it once was."

Bull released a slow breath. "We shall bury her in a place of honor. She shall be among the greatest of us. We who loved her best."

Deer turned on him, his eyes wild like sparks. "No. Burying her deep in the ground is what her mother would have wanted."

Turtle rested a hand on his younger brother. "But, Deer—"

"No, I say!" Deer lowered his head as if he had antlers and was about to charge. "Her mother wanted to be the fairest, but Snow White retains that honor, even in death. Instead, let us build a coffin with a glass top." His eyes narrowed. "It shall serve as a reminder to us. She did not betray us when her mother threatened her."

The dwarfs mimicked Turtle's gesture, each placing his own hand on Deer's back.

They spent the following day building the coffin, exerting themselves to their limits, creating not a box but a work of art. Through the night, hidden from everyone, they elevated her coffin and placed it atop a rarefied platform. They set it in a grove on their property but a distance from their house. Deer had wanted to guard it. The rest of the dwarfs tried to talk him out of it, but he persisted. They surrendered to his wishes, but he knew one day he would have to leave Snow White unattended.

◆ ◆ ◆

Deer stood in the light rain next to the coffin containing his lady, a girl above all other girls. He didn't want to ever leave her. He would rather remain here for the rest of his life, waiting for a miracle, which he hoped would come soon.

He had never told his family the details of what he'd witnessed the day Snow White bit into the apple. Perhaps he would confess it in the future, but for now, her words were too traumatic. He had failed her, and he was ashamed to admit it. She had sacrificed her life for theirs. Ironic, given all the talk of their protection of her.

Deer settled his fingers on the glass lid to the coffin. Snow White didn't show any signs of decomposition. When they lifted her inside the enclosure, her limbs remained flexible, contrary to any corpses Deer had moved in his life. A good sign, surely? Why had her invulnerability not worked with the apple? These questions plagued the youngest dwarf, who, unlike his brothers, hadn't accepted her demise.

Suddenly, someone emerged from the underbrush and Deer grabbed his knife, pointing it at the intruder. Rabbit was due to replace him in a couple of hours. Deer often spent the nights at sentry for Snow White. Only an enemy would approach at this time of his watch.

But he was wrong. Rabbit stepped from between two trees and stopped short of the blade. Tensed for action, the guardian dwarf lowered his shoulders relieved but then flashed a grimace of irritation. "What are ye doing here?"

"Strangers are at home. They have been asking questions about Snow White."

Alarm consumed Deer. "Ye have told them nothing, I hope."

Rabbit twitched. "Do ye take your brothers for fools? But our lady's friend, the woman in red, is among them."

"Are ye sure 'tis her?"

Rabbit gestured at the coffin. "I am sure. She wept bitterly at the news of her demise. But I have more news. A man accompanied the women in red, and he knows everything about our lady. Deer, he knows about the coffin."

Deer took a step forward. "Impossible. We told no one."

"I tell ye, he knows. He does not believe she is dead."

The youngest dwarf started at the news. Rabbit continued, "We have offered them shelter at the cottage. Ye go back and I will stay here. Guide them here if ye think they are not villains."

Deer hugged his brother. "Thank ye. I will be back."

Deer left, sprinting through the circle of trees to the hills beyond. Perhaps these strangers could help. For the first time since Snow White had died three days before, Deer wondered if he might be called Dear once again.

AFTERWORD

The fun doesn't have to stop here. If you want to learn more about Kingdom and its inhabitants, read "Kingdom Come", and "On Earth, As It Is", where the adventures continue. The stories in Kingdom's Advent are prequels to these novels.

Furthermore, please check out jimdorantales.com. You will find more short stories of Kingdom including the ongoing stories of characters included in this collection. I have a page devoted to each of the short stories within this book, giving you, valued reader, some extra information associated with each tale.

If you'd be so kind, feel free to leave a review of this collection.

If you would like to contact me directly, please email me at jim.doran.author@gmail.com.

ACKNOWLEDGEMENT

The author would like to acknowledge the following people who helped bring these stories alive.

God - Of course!

Daniel Johnson - His art captures the very essence of Kingdom. Daniel created the cover, the map, and all interior art.

G. Miki Hayden - A spectacular editor whose guidance makes Kingdom stories soar with the wyverns.

Eliza Luckey - A treasured critique partner who guided my friend "Coal" not once but twice.

Kristiana Sfirlea - For bringing attention to my short stories from your blog, many thanks.

Baptiste Pinson - A remarkable critique partner who reviewed early versions of the stories.

Paxton Doran - My youngest critique partner who keeps me on the straight and narrow.

And, of course, Hope. On those tough days when I want to run away to Kingdom, she reminds me that earth is a special place all its own.

ABOUT THE AUTHOR

Jim Doran

Jim Doran is a genre author who enjoys transporting his readers to unique destinations filled with wonder and spectacle. Within his novels, you will find fascinating locations that include the wooden castles of Nor, the diminutive trees of Faerie Forest, or the treacherous alleys of Exile. To learn more about Jim and his writing, visit jimdorantales.com.

THE KINGDOM FANTASY SERIES

Kingdom, a fairy tale realm of spells and magical creatures, is a world where both grand adventures and chance incidents take place. The residents may seem familiar and their stories well known, but don't be fooled. Kingdom holds many surprises.

Kingdom Come: A Fantasy Novel

When Harold Tray is transported to the fairy tale world of Kingdom, he meets Planet the pixie and embarks on an epic quest to reunite five queens.

On Earth, As It Is: A Kingdom Fantasy Novel

Three years after the events of Kingdom Come, a friend arrives to tell Harold someone has abducted the five queens of Kingdom.

www.ingramcontent.com/pod-product-compliance
Lightning Source LLC
Chambersburg PA
CBHW030544130626
46552CB00006B/2407